AR Quiz # 153699
BL: 4.1
AR pts - 5.0

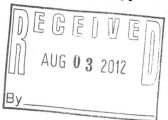

W9-BCD-017

RECEIVED
AUG 0 3 2012
By_____

PENELOPE
CRUMB

PHILOMEL BOOKS

A division of Penguin Young Readers Group.

Published by The Penguin Group.

Penguin Group (USA) Inc., 375 Hudson Street, New York, NY 10014, U.S.A.

Penguin Group (Canada), 90 Eglinton Avenue East, Suite 700, Toronto, Ontario M4P 2Y3, Canada (a division of Pearson Penguin Canada Inc.).

Penguin Books Ltd, 80 Strand, London WC2R 0RL, England.

Penguin Ireland, 25 St Stephen's Green, Dublin 2, Ireland (a division of Penguin Books Ltd).

Penguin Group (Australia), 250 Camberwell Road, Camberwell, Victoria 3124, Australia (a division of Pearson Australia Group Pty Ltd).

Penguin Books India Pvt Ltd, 11 Community Centre, Panchsheel Park, New Delhi—110 017, India.

Penguin Group (NZ), 67 Apollo Drive, Rosedale, Auckland 0632, New Zealand (a division of Pearson New Zealand Ltd).

Penguin Books (South Africa) (Pty) Ltd, 24 Sturdee Avenue, Rosebank, Johannesburg 2196, South Africa.

Penguin Books Ltd, Registered Offices: 80 Strand, London WC2R 0RL, England.

Edited by Jill Santopolo.   Design by Semadar Megged.
Text set in 14.5-point Fournier MT Std.
Library of Congress Cataloging-in-Publication Data
Stout, Shawn K.   Penelope Crumb / Shawn Stout.   p. cm.
Summary: Fourth-grader Penelope Crumb's large nose leads to a family discovery.
[1. Nose—Fiction. 2. Families—Fiction. 3. Grandfathers—Fiction.] I. Title.
PZ7.S88838Pe 2012   [Fic]—dc23   2011017478
ISBN 978-0-399-25728-5
3 5 7 9 10 8 6 4 2

PENELOPE CRUMB

SHAWN K. STOUT

with art by VALERIA DOCAMPO

PHILOMEL BOOKS
An Imprint of Penguin Group (USA) Inc.

For Opal, for Albert A. Beck,
and for big noses everywhere.

1.

Miss Stunkel's art class is my All-Time Favorite. Don't get me wrong, the rest of fourth grade is all right, I guess. But for me, drawing is like wiggling my toes in the ocean. It just feels good.

I take out my No. 2 Hard drawing pencil from my red metal toolbox and carefully study my best friend Patsy's face.

"Hmmm." I squint my left eye and pucker my lips, which is what famous artists do when they are concentrating hard. I know that because I saw a cartoon about Leonardo da Vinci once, who was a very, very famous artist who lived a very, very long time ago (he's dead now, like all famous artists are), and that's just what he did when he painted. I want to be a famous artist, too, but not a dead one.

"What?" says Patsy.

"I'm trying to decide which side of your face is the best one," I tell her.

"They're the exact same, Penelope," she says.

"Are not." But then I add real quick so she won't be mad, "It's okay, Patsy, *no*body's face is that way."

She gives me a look. I know that look because I'm real good at telling what different kinds of faces mean. It's an artist's job to notice things like that. Her face says, You Are Truly Making That Up.

Patsy doesn't know anything about art. I mean, nothing. She wouldn't know Leonardo da Vinci if he handed her a paintbrush and said, "How do you do, little darling?" But that's okay, because singing is her thing.

When Patsy was born, her mom and dad must

have known she would be a good singer because they named her Patsy Cline. After the famous country-western singer also named Patsy Cline (she's dead now, too). Only, Patsy Cline (my very best friend, not the famous country-western singer who is dead) is her first name. Her full name is Patsy Cline Roberta Watson. Which is the longest name of anybody I've ever met. Even longer than Leonardo da Vinci's. (I've never actually met him on account of you know . . .)

So we just call her Patsy.

"I'll do this side," I say. "Because the other side has dirt on it."

"Better stop your fibbing."

"True blue," I say. "It's right here." I poke my finger at Patsy's smudgy cheek. And then I get a whiff. "Mustard?"

Patsy wipes at her cheek with the back of her hand. "Pretzels for breakfast."

"Hold still," I say.

Patsy makes her lips into a straight line.

"Wow, Patsy, you look just like Mona Lisa."

She raises her eyebrow like she thinks I'm Queen of the Fibbers, but she keeps her mouth straight. "This is as bad as posing to have my picture taken for All-Star Kids," she says without moving her lips. "You're coming to my audition on Sunday, aren't you?" I tell her that I am and to stop talking so I can finish.

"It didn't take me this long to draw you!" she says.

"Patsy," I say, being as patient as I can be, "do you think that Miss Mona Lisa told Mister Leonardo da Vinci to hurry up?"

"I bet she would if she had a thousand-legger crawling down her neck. Or if she ate some spoiled ham the night before that gave her the runs." Patsy sure has a way of putting things.

After I get through with Patsy's mouth, I draw her frizzed-out hair. It's the color of chocolate cherry fudge, and she sure has a mess of it. Her curls sprout every which way on her head. "Tuck your hair behind your ear," I tell her.

Patsy cups her hands over her ears and then pulls her hair forward to cover them. "What for?"

"So I can draw your ear. You know, the thing that's on the side of your head."

"Never mind my ear," she says. "My hair is my best feature."

I give her a look that says, That's a Good One. I know for a fact that Patsy wishes she could get the curls out of her hair but good. Especially when Patsy's mom attacks them with bobby pins and hair gel before singing contests just so she can get her cowgirl hat to fit. But I decide to keep this nugget to myself and keep on drawing.

"Are you done yet?"

"Almost." I draw her eyebrow. I can only see one, since I am drawing just one side of her face. (The side without the mustard.)

Her eyebrow is like a furry caterpillar that might curl up in the palm of my hand. It is so cute, I name it. Marge.

I am right in the middle of drawing Marge the Caterpillar when Patsy leans over my desk to try to get a peek at my drawing. But I quickly cover it with my arms so she can't see. "You're not supposed to look yet," I tell her. "Remember?"

"Okay, everyone." Miss Stunkel taps her desk. "Who would like to go first?"

Fast as a flash, I finish furry Marge and then raise my hand high.

Miss Stunkel peers around the room and touches her Thursday Lizard pin on her blouse. Thursday Lizard is plain and silver and not as good as Friday Lizard, which has red stones for eyeballs. But Patsy Cline hates them all because she's allergic to things with tails. "Well, I don't see many hands."

I raise my hand higher, but Miss Stunkel keeps on looking. I think she might need glasses.

I raise my hand even higher still, so high that my fingers begin to tingle. "Oooh." The tingles start creeping down my arm. I see Miss Stunkel look my way.

Then she looks right at me.

I flash her a smile that says, Look How Quiet

and Good I Am, So Pretty Please with Sprinkles on Top, Will You Pick Me? Miss Stunkel smiles back. But I know that smile. It says, I've Already Called on You Several Times Today, So Let's Give Someone Else a Turn.

"Patsy Cline, why don't you go first," Miss Stunkel says.

Well then. I shake the tingles out of my arm. Miss Stunkel always picks kids who aren't even raising their hands. I think it must be something teachers learn in How to Be the Kind of Teacher That Kids Don't Like School, because last year my third-grade teacher, Mr. Adler, did the same thing.

Patsy slumps her shoulders, and I can tell by the look on her face that she is not one bit happy about having to go first. I try to give her a look like the one my mom gives me at the doctor's when I'm about to get a shot: It Will Be So Fast You Won't Even Feel It.

Patsy hugs the drawing to her stomach and heads to the front of the room.

I look from Patsy to my drawing of Patsy's face and decide that Marge could use a bit more fur. I add a couple more hairs on Marge and then I hear Patsy say, "This is my drawing of my best friend, Penelope Crumb." I put down my pencil and give Patsy a big grin. But then I see her drawing of me.

Good gravy. I'm not 100 percent sure, but I think I stop breathing right then and there. I might even go dead for a second. Maybe two. But somehow I get alive again, and when I do, Patsy is still holding up that drawing.

Don't get me wrong. For a singer, Patsy drew my hair, eye, ear, and chin just fine and dandy. But that nose. *My* nose. Is. Humungous.

In the next row, Angus Meeker laughs. And for a second, I think he's laughing at Patsy's bad talent for drawing: *Ha-ha, that's a real mess of a picture. Patsy drew a potato sticking out of poor old Penelope's face!* But then he looks right at me, that awful Angus Meeker does, and he says, "Yep, looks just like her." Which gets other people going.

I give Miss Stunkel a look that says, Aren't You Going to Say Something about This?

But Miss Stunkel just smiles like Patsy is Mister Leonardo da Vinci himself. "Very nice," she says to Patsy, making a big deal out of the *very*. And then Miss Stunkel says something else. "Your drawing bears a remarkable resemblance to Penelope."

Which just about makes me go dead again.

2.

Nose thoughts, GREAT BIG ONES, are in my head for the rest of the day. And when I get home to our apartment, I let loose with a howl. "Mom!"

"Back here!" she hollers.

Down the long hallway to the back of our apartment, I find Mom perched at our dryer. She's been using it as a desk ever since it broke last year. She won't get it fixed, like most everything else that's broken-down, and so we dry our clothes at the Laundromat or sometimes on our tiny porch if it's not raining.

The top of the dryer/desk is cluttered with glass jars stuffed full of felt-tip pens, No. 2 Hard drawing pencils that I sometimes borrow, and paintbrushes that Mom says are made from real horse's hair. "What do you think?" she says, pulling her feet out of the dryer door and holding up her sketch pad. "And tell the truth."

It's a drawing of a heart. And I don't mean a Valentine's Day heart. Not the kind that looks like this: ♥. I mean the kind of heart that's inside of you, with blood and veins and all kinds of creepy stuff like that. I stare at the heart but all I can see is the nose in Patsy's drawing. "Very nice," I say to Mom, just like Miss Stunkel said it, making a big deal out of the *very*.

Mom eyeballs the drawing and then reaches for her eraser. "I think the left ventricle looks too big." Mom is going to school to be an insides artist. She draws people's insides for books that doctors read. I don't know why doctors would want to see those kinds of pictures in books because I'm pretty sure they see a lot of that creepy stuff in real life.

She blows the eraser bits from her drawing pad and asks, "Anything interesting happen at school today?" without looking up. This is one of her Regulars for when I get home. I usually answer with a Regular of my own: "Nope." And then we will go on about our business. But today is no day for Regulars.

"I died."

That gets her attention. Mom drops the eraser and it goes bouncing off behind the dryer/desk. She spins on her stool to face me and I know by the red blotches on her face that she is not happy about what I said. "Penelope Rae," she says, in a way that makes my name sound like a gross body part. Large Intestine, for example.

Mom doesn't much like it when I talk about dead things. I think it's on account of the fact that I have a dead father. Graveyard Dead. But for someone who draws people's insides, you'd think dead things wouldn't be such a big deal.

I quick move off the subject of me dying and spill out the awful story about what happened today from beginning to end. I make sure I use the right words to describe the nose in Patsy's drawing: *gigantic, enormous, huge, extremely large . . . COLOSSAL!*

The blotches start to fade and her eyes get big when I say COLOSSAL like she's impressed that I know such a word. But I haven't even gotten to the worst part. That's when I tell her how Angus Meeker laughed and how Miss Stunkel said that Patsy's drawing was a remarkable resemblance of me.

Mom twists her long hair on top of her head and sticks in a pencil to hold the knot. Then she puts her hand on my shoulder and gives me a face that says, You Probably Aren't Going to Like What I'm about to Tell You.

"What?"

"What's going on?" says Terrible, from behind me, making me jump.

Oh brother. "Nothing." I squeeze my eyes shut and make a wish that he would get on his spaceship already. Around the time he turned fourteen, my brother, Terrence, was snatched by aliens. When they brought him back, he was different. *Alien* different. Terrible.

"Doesn't sound like nothing, dorkus," Terrible says.

See what I mean? Ever since the snatching I've been keeping a list of all of his alien traits so that one day I can report him to NASA. Name-calling is Number 3.

"Penelope," Mom says, "I'm afraid you have a Crumb nose."

"What is that?" I say. "And why does that make you afraid?"

"She means from Dad's side of the family, jeez," says Terrible, taking off his bomber jacket. His stinky cologne smells like fishing worms mixed with orange sherbet and furniture polish (Number 5). "Don't you know anything?"

I give him a look that says, I Hope the Aliens Come Back for You Soon. Then I say to Mom, "I have Dad's nose?" Which wouldn't really be a bad thing, on account of the fact that Dad died when I was just a baby, and I don't have anything of his except for a shoehorn and that beat-up old toolbox with rusty corners that I take with me everywhere.

"Well, not exactly," she says, staring at my nose from different angles like it was a creepy inside she was about to draw. "I mean, a little bit, you do. But you have a more pronounced onion."

"Onion!" I say. Onions are the cruelest of all vegetables because they 1) smell awful, 2) make you cry for no reason, and 3) look like worms when you fry them up in a skillet. Onions are bad enough on your supper plate, but in your nose!

Mom says rhinion—not onion!—and then points to the middle of her own nose. "The area right here. You have a little bump."

I run my finger along the top of my nose. "I don't feel anything. What's the bump there for?"

Mom shrugs. "That's just the way some noses are."

"Yours isn't," I say to her. Then I point at the alien. "Neither is his."

"Your grandpa Felix has one." The blotches on her face are back.

"How can you not know you have a big nose?" says Terrible, shaking his alien head. "It's in the middle of your face."

I try to look at my nose, but my eyes go crossed. "A nose isn't like elbows or knees that you can just look at anytime you want to and there they are, you know." I show him both elbows and pull up my pant leg so he can see my knee.

"There are these rectangular things around here, Penelope," he says. "They're called mirrors. You should look in one every once in a while."

Aliens think they are so smart. There aren't any mirrors in the laundry room, so I run down the hall and into our living room to see myself. Terrible's footsteps are right behind me.

In front of the mirror, I tilt and turn my head every which way to try to see my nose from all directions. Straight on, it looks like it always has, not really that big or different. But it's hard to get a good long look at the thing from the side.

How long has my nose been big? If it's an artist's job to notice things, like red eyeballs on Friday Lizard, dirt on a shoestring, or a caterpillary eyebrow, then how did I miss this?

Terrible says, "It's pretty much always been big, in case you were wondering." Alien mind reading (Number 6) really gets on my nerves. "Remember when we went swimming at that lake that time and you had to wear a snorkeling mask for grown-ups because the kid size was too tight?"

"I thought that was because of my big head," I say.

"Or that you can't eat an ice cream cone without it getting all over your nose?"

"Good gravy. That happens to everybody on account of the fact that your mouth lives here and your nose lives one floor up," I say, pointing to them both. "Doesn't it? Happen to everyone, I mean?"

He shakes his head at me in the mirror. "Nope," he says with a smile that's all puppy dogs and rainbows.

My word. "Well, since you know so much," I sputter, "how come nobody's ever said anything before?"

Terrible doesn't even take any time to think about this one. "There are so many things about you that are weird, Penelope. If I had to point them all out, it would take me the rest of my life."

I wonder if Mister Leonardo da Vinci ever had a brother who was an alien.

3.

Littie Maple is knocking at my bedroom door. I keep my face pressed down on my drawing pad and tell her to get in here pronto because I am in need of some help. She does. Which is the good thing about Littie: She's a doer.

Littie lives in the apartment across the hall, but she spends more time in ours because she's a Lonely Only. Which is what she calls herself on account of the fact that she is an only child and is homeschooled and doesn't have a TV. "What do you have your face on that paper for?"

"Trace it, would you?" I say, shoving a pencil at her.

She steps over the Heap on the floor and kneels beside me. She doesn't ask why or what for or anything like that, she just grips the pencil and starts tracing. Her tongue wags in the corner of her mouth as she steers the pencil. When she gets to my forehead, she clamps down on her tongue with her teeth like she's keeping it from running off to Texas.

"There," she says when she's through. She stands up and claps her hands. "That's a keeper." Littie is eleven, which is almost two years older than I am, but most people think she's younger on account of the fact that she's on the short side. (But don't ever say anything about her being short because she will bend your fingers back until you say you're sorry like you mean it.)

I look at the drawing. Mostly I look at my nose. It's sticking out like it's trying to get somebody's attention. And here's the thing: You have to admire a nose like that.

I imagine Mister Leonardo da Vinci would be happy to draw a nose such as mine. If he saw it, he would grab his pencils and say, "Drawing a nose of this size would use up all of my pencils, and my hand would surely get a cramp. But it would be worth it, yes indeed, lucky stars, it would." Because that is how dead artists talk.

"Do me next," Littie says.

I flip to a new page on my drawing pad and press Littie's tiny head to it, then I trace. When I'm done, I hold them up side by side. Littie's nose has no bumps and is round and short, sort of like the letter C if it had swallowed a coat hanger.

My nose, on the other hand, is a Big Rock Candy Mountain. I draw a tiny person on skis right at the top. The tip of my nose is more pointy than round. And that's a good thing because that skier can go flying off the end instead of tumbling into my mouth. Blech.

"It's a Crumb nose," I inform Littie. "From my dad's side of the family. Whose nose do you have?"

Littie shrugs. "Everybody says I'm the spitting

image of my momma, but when I get into trouble, Momma says I've got my pap's disposition."

While I think about whose disposition I have, I catch her staring. "What?"

"Nothing. I'm just having a look," she says. "All this talk about your nose makes me notice it more now."

"That's all right," I tell her, sticking it in the air. "I don't mind."

Littie looks it over real close. So close that I can tell she had bologna for lunch. "Don't you mind having a boy's nose?" she asks.

"What do you mean?"

"You said it's from your dad's side of the family," she says. "You know, the *boy* side." She sticks her tongue out of her bologna-smelling mouth like she's going to upchuck.

Which makes me say this not-so-nice thing: "I'd rather have a boy's nose than a pea-size head."

"Who has a pea-size head?" she says with her hands on her hips.

"Nobody," I say, shrugging. "Definitely not you,

Littie Maple." If she doesn't know she has a pea-size head, I'm sure not going to be the one to tell her.

Boy's nose or not, I really wish I did have my dad's, on account of the fact that besides the tool-box and the shoehorn and some pictures, there's hardly any proof that Dad was ever here. I used to pretend that he was just away on a trip, like Littie's dad is sometimes, and that he'd be right here wait-ing for me when I got home from school, asking for his toolbox back. But Mom says I'm getting too old for pretending.

Terrible sticks his head in my door. "Hey, wom-bat. Mom wants me to tell you to get your dirty clothes together. She's doing laundry."

"I don't have any," I say, drawing goggles on my skier.

He points to the Heap. "What about all that?"

"That's not dirty." I pick up a shirt from the pile and sniff it. "See?"

Littie takes a whiff, nods, and says, "Smells like hamburgers. I'm just saying."

I sniff my shirt again, and somehow it *does* smell like hamburgers. Delicious ones that we sometimes get at the White Star Luncheonette. I hold the shirt out for Terrible to smell, but he shoves my hand away and tells me I'm both gross and disgusting.

Well then. Aliens don't like the smell of hamburgers. That's going on my list. I throw the shirt back on the Heap and get back to my drawing.

"Fine," he says. "I'm telling Mom."

"Fine," I say, shrugging and sticking my nose in the air. But when he turns to leave, I follow. "Wait. What are you going to tell her?" I'm close behind him, down the hall. Littie is right behind me with the shirt in her hands.

Terrible comes to a stop beside Mom at the kitchen table. "She won't pick up her clothes."

Tattle-telling alien.

"Penelope." Mom keeps her eyes on a family photo album that's open in front of her.

"Tell her about the hamburgers," Littie whispers as she shoves the shirt at me. But I give her a look that says, Now Is Not the Time for Meat.

"What are you looking at?" I ask Mom.

Terrible answers, "Pictures, duh. What does it look like?"

Mom sighs and tells the alien he ought to be nice to his sister. I say, "Yes, he *ought*." Even though I know he won't ought. I slide into the chair next to Mom and lean in close as she turns the pages. My nose twitches. "Where's Grandpa Felix?"

As my family goes by in pages, Littie squeezes in beside me and chews on her thumbnail. Mom points to a picture. "There," she says.

I've seen pictures of Grandpa Felix before, but my dad is in most of them. So, I never really paid much attention to the grandpa part.

"And that's your nose," Terrible says, smirking.

"*My* grandpa's got hair growing inside of his nose," says Littie. "In his ears, too. Looks like spider legs."

I give her a look that says, What Does That Have

to Do with the Color of Mud? She says, "You've got a grandpa nose. I'm just saying."

I nudge her with my elbow. "Maybe so. But my nose doesn't have spider legs." Then I stick my finger up in there just to be sure.

"Not yet it doesn't," Littie says, nudging me back. "I'm just saying."

I look at the picture up close, nose to nose. No spider legs, thank lucky stars. When you're Graveyard Dead, I bet there are spider legs, real ones, in your nose. And other places, too. Then my eyes go to the smiling face right beside Grandpa. "I wonder why Dad's nose isn't the same."

Littie rattles on about how she doesn't have some mole the shape of a lima bean on her neck even though her momma and grandmother do, but I'm barely listening because I'm tracing my dad's nose with my finger. His nose is thin and regular looking, and makes him look like the kind of person who would let a stray dog have a lick of a lollipop, just because.

Grandpa looks like the kind of person who would call the dog catcher, but I'm not sure if that's because of our nose or something else. "When Grandpa Felix was alive . . ."

Mom clears her throat. "Penelope Rae." (Colon.)

"What?"

"Grandpa Felix is not dead. Why would you think he's dead? Why do you *always* think that everybody is dead?"

"I don't know," I tell her. "A lot of the time they just are."

Mom says she hasn't talked to Grandpa Felix in a long time, not since I was a baby, not since Dad got sick. But then I want to know, "Well, if you haven't talked to him, how do you know Grandpa Felix isn't Graveyard Dead?"

Mom gives me a look that says, If You Don't Stop Talking about Dead Things, I'm Going to Pull My Hair Out by the Roots.

So I do, for now. Because Mom looks a lot better not bald.

4.

Nighttime is the best time to think about dead people, because in the dark and hush quiet, it's easy to imagine my Graveyard Dead dad patting my foot under the covers and saying, "Oh, little darling. Oh, my heart."

But this night, when I'm supposed to be asleep, I get to thinking a lot about Grandpa Felix not being Graveyard Dead. Why don't we talk to him if he's not dead? And if he's not dead, why doesn't he talk to us?

Me and Terrible asked about him before, I know

so, but Mom always said he was just gone. Just gone like Gram Trudy, my dad's mother, who I never met. Just gone like Dad.

That's what I thought, anyhow. But maybe there are reasons other than being dead for somebody to be gone.

Terrible's bedroom is across the hall from mine. His door is covered in stickers that say things like NO TRESPASSING! and DANGER! KEEP OUT! and ENTER AT YOUR OWN RISK! with lots of exclamation points on account of the fact that aliens really don't like visitors. The door is open a crack, so I poke my head inside. All of the lights are out except for one by his bed, and I can see half of his face lit up in the dark. He's got one eye open, but that doesn't mean anything when it comes to aliens (Number 7). "Are you asleep?" I whisper.

He gets up, and two steps later he's at the door in front of me. "Did you think Grandpa Felix was dead?" I ask him through the crack.

He looks at me for a second and says, "Yes,

dork." Then he closes the door on me, and my nose nearly gets pinched off.

"Me too," I say quietly, after the door closes. I run my finger over the ENTER AT YOUR OWN RISK! sticker. Of all the dead people I know, Grandpa Felix is the only one who's turned out to be alive. The only one. And I think it's too bad that I don't know him.

Down the hall, Mom's room is all dark. She's snoring, and it sounds like slurping chocolate milk through a straw when you get to the bottom of the cup—*cwuuurgh!*—which I'm not allowed to do on account of the fact that it's not polite. But *cwuuurgh!* when you're sleeping must be different from *cwuuurgh!* when you've got a straw, because Mom is allowed to do it all the time.

I climb in bed beside Mom and hug one of her extra pillows to my chest. It smells like cinnamon spice. Then real gentle, I touch the side of Mom's face with my finger, right next to her ear. This is something I do to see how many touches

I can get in before she wakes up. Twenty-four is my world record. (Note: Do not try this game with aliens.)

I get to eighteen when she sits up in bed and says, "Margarine!" like she's been dreaming about groceries.

So I say, "Butter!" like we're playing that game where one person gives a clue about something and the other person has to guess what it is.

But Mom must not be in the mood to play that game right now, because she looks at me, rubs the sleep out of her eyeballs, and says, "What in the world are you doing?"

"Nothing," I say, sitting on my finger.

She props herself up on a pillow and yawns. "You weren't doing that touching thing again, were you?"

"Nope."

"Penelope Rae." (Gallbladder.)

"Why did you always say that Grandpa Felix was gone when he was not gone?" I ask.

"What?" says Mom. I repeat the question, and she says, "Do we have to talk about this now?"

"You said he was gone," I say. "You said so. But he's not dead and I have his nose and still I don't know him."

"I never said Grandpa Felix was dead," she says.

"You never said he was *not* dead."

"Penelope Crumb."

"Mom Crumb," I say. "So, where is he if he's not dead?"

She yawns and then rolls over on her side so that I'm talking to the back of her head. "Where's who?"

"Grandpa Felix. The not-dead grandpa that we've been talking about." I poke my finger at the back of her head to wake up her brains.

"Stop doing that," she says once they get awake. She looks at me over her shoulder. "I don't know where he is. I lost track of him over the years, but the last time we spoke he was living in Simmons."

"Simmons? That's where Nanny and Pop-Pop used to live."

When she doesn't say anything, I give her brains another poke. She turns over then and grabs my cinnamon-spice-smelling pillow right out from under me. "Go to sleep," she says, pointing to the door. "Now." And then she pulls the pillow over her head.

5.

When I get to school, Miss Stunkel's got our drawings hanging above the chalkboard. This would normally be a good thing because famous artists like Leonardo da Vinci have their drawings stuck up on walls for lots of people to see. But this is not a good thing on account of the fact that Patsy's bad drawing of me is up there.

I tell my eyeballs not to look at it, and try to get them to look at Miss Stunkel's Friday lizard pin or the "Math is stupid" that somebody wrote on the corner of my desk in permanent marker.

(Which was not me even though I also think that math is stupid.) But my eyeballs don't listen, and they keep looking at Patsy's bad drawing of me.

The next thing I know, Miss Stunkel is saying my name. Twice.

I put a look on my face that says, I Really, Really Have Been Paying Attention to Every Word You Have Been Saying. (Even though I really, really have not.)

But it doesn't work because Miss Stunkel says, "We are on page twenty-two . . . where are you?"

Everybody laughs, except for me and Patsy Cline. "Umm," I say, looking at Patsy for help. But Patsy is staring up at Friday Lizard like her tongue is starting to swell.

Miss Stunkel says, "Eyes on your book." And that's when I know I have to fix that drawing if I'm going to make it through the rest of the day without Miss Stunkel sending a note home.

So, during recess, when everybody is outside playing and Miss Stunkel is eating her pickled ham sandwich (because that's what teachers eat) in the teachers' lounge, I sneak back into the classroom. I am an excellent sneaker. Stepping onto a chair, I pull a No. 2 Hard drawing pencil and eraser from my back pocket and get to work on my nose. And when I'm done, I can practically hear Mister Leonardo say: "Yes indeed, a mighty fine work. Much improved."

And he would be right.

After recess, my eyeballs have no trouble paying attention to Miss Stunkel when she scribbles on the chalkboard. Especially when she pulls out a plaid hat with earflaps from her pocket and slides it on. Like Miss Stunkel's all of a sudden worried that the chalk dust might make the faces in the drawings start sneezing on her head.

I give Patsy Cline a look that says, Miss Stunkel Has Gone and Lost Her Marbles. Patsy's eyes get wide, and the next thing I know, Miss Stunkel's got a magnifying glass up to her face. "Who am I?" she says.

"You're Miss Stunkel," says Angus Meeker.

I roll my eyes and try my hardest to hold back a *duh*. Then I raise my hand.

"Well, of course," says Miss Stunkel. She puts the magnifying glass real close to her face now, which makes her eyeball look so big and bulgy that I can see the red squiggly lines in the white parts. "But who am I *now*?"

I raise my hand higher still.

"I am a detective," she says, without giving me a chance. "And you all are going to be detectives, too. I want you to do some digging and find out about your family history." She hands Angus a box of small magnifying glasses and tells him to pass them around. "Maybe your family came here from another country, or maybe your family has special celebrations or traditions."

Angus Meeker tries to hand me a magnifying glass that's got a crack in it, but I push his hand away and take a good one from the box. I hold it up to my eye, and through the looking glass everything is great big: my toolbox, the Hairy Stink Eye that Angus is giving me, the hole in Miss Stunkel's panty hose.

Then Miss Stunkel pounds on the chalkboard at what she's written:

Become a Detective!

1. Discover what you don't know about your family. Find out about your family's traditions and customs.
2. Make a coat of arms for your family. Use pictures or drawings to show your family's history.

"You will take what you've learned about your family," she says, "and make a coat of arms."

"An arm coat?" I say. "You mean with elbows and everything?" Angus Meeker laughs, but I know he doesn't know any more about it than I do.

"Penelope Crumb," says Miss Stunkel, "you know my rule. Pupils in my classroom must raise their hands if they want to say something."

I raise my hand like a good pupil and say, "Whose arms are they? And how do you put them on a coat?" Because that seems like kind of a creepy thing to do.

Miss Stunkel takes a deep breath and closes her eyes. She looks just like Mom does when we're halfway to the store and she realizes she left her grocery list on the counter. Then Miss Stunkel opens her eyes again. She explains that a coat of arms is not a coat made of arms or elbows at all. It's a picture, or a bunch of pictures, usually drawn on the shape of a shield, that show things about a family. A family's history, for example, she says.

Well. Somehow that doesn't seem as good.

"And put some time and thought into this art project," says Miss Stunkel, "because one of your coats of arms will be selected for display at the Portwaller-in-Bloom Spring Festival. So make it pop."

Good gravy. If I won, lots of people would come to see what I made. Just like Leonardo.

Right away I start thinking. I tap my finger on

my head to wake up my brains. My family is the kind that doesn't have any traditions. "Does eating ham-and-egg sandwiches all the time count?" I ask.

Miss Stunkel looks around the room and says, "Someone is speaking, but I don't see a hand raised."

I am that someone. So I put both of my hands in the air and keep them there in case I forget again. "What if you don't have any traditions or costumes?"

"Customs, not costumes," says Miss Stunkel. And then she says that the purpose of the arm coat is to find out things you don't know about your family. "That's why you are going to be detectives."

Then my brains really start to work. Because I think about how I didn't know I had a big nose that belongs to my not-dead grandpa Felix. And if I didn't know that, there might be other things I don't know about.

Like, maybe Dad isn't Graveyard Dead at all. Maybe he's a secret agent who is undercover in some faraway place, like, as a taxi driver in one of those countries where cars have to stop for sheep that can cross the street by themselves, and we have to think he's dead. At least for now. Until he can come home.

Or maybe, just maybe, I have a secret aunt that nobody knows about who is really a queen from a faraway island with coconut trees and kangaroos. And maybe that island is full of people with big noses. She probably has been looking for me and my nose for a long time. So she can make me a warrior princess.

In her kingdom, a big nose means royalty. Real warrior-princess material. And she will invite me to spend the whole entire summer with her. "Would you like a fancy lemonade drink with a tiny umbrella?" a butler would ask me while I wiggle my toes in the ocean. "Yes, as a matter of fact, I would like that very much," I would reply, "just as soon as I take a swim alongside these purple polka-dotted fish with orange lips."

Then a high-pitch shriek from Patsy Cline interrupts my island thoughts.

Miss Stunkel clutches her chest, and says, "Mercy. What is the matter?"

Patsy Cline, being the good pupil that she is, has her hand raised. Then she points at the wall and yells, "Somebody graffitied my drawing. Look!"

Everybody looks where she's pointing. Angus Meeker's mouth falls open and he says, "Whoa, man oh day!" But I don't see what all the fuss is about.

Miss Stunkel turns purple in the face. She clears her throat and says, "Who is responsible for this? I demand to know immediately."

I raise my hand, but Miss Stunkel doesn't call on me. Instead, she looks at me like she's sorry. Sorry for what, I don't know. I drop my hand.

Miss Stunkel wraps her fingers tight around

Friday Lizard. "I'm waiting," she says. "Who did this to Patsy Cline's drawing? Who is the graffiti artist that made Penelope's nose look so . . . umm, so . . . like that?"

Graffiti artist? I look from Miss Stunkel to the nose in Patsy's drawing, the one I fixed to look like it really does on my real face: bigger and with Grandpa Felix's bump. I even drew on the skier with her goggles and everything.

"Who?" says Miss Stunkel again, turning purple-er.

"Me. I'm the graffiti artist," I say. "What's a graffiti artist?"

Miss Stunkel's eyes get so big that I'm afraid her eyelids will disappear inside her head where her brains live. And then I realize that I forgot to raise my hand this time. So I do. Both of them.

But it must be too late, because Miss Stunkel's fingers are still clamped around Friday Lizard. And I worry that her eyeballs are going to turn red like his. "You did this?" she says.

"Yep." I wave my hands at her so she's sure to see that this time I remembered.

"Penelope Crumb," she says. "I'd like a Word with you after school."

By the look on her face, I know she's not going to let me pick the Word.

6.

Miss Stunkel's Word turns out to be a Sentence. One with two parts to it. "Penelope Crumb, I'm very disappointed in you, and I don't very much like to be disappointed in my pupils because it gives me wrinkles." Which it really does.

"I know," I say, pointing to her forehead. "Sorry about all of those."

She gives me a look like she doesn't know what I'm talking about. But if she doesn't know her forehead is chockful of wrinkles, then I am not going to be the one to tell her. "Never mind" is what I say and then nothing else.

Miss Stunkel sends a note home. But before she hands it over, she tells me that the note isn't meant for my eyeballs and so I'm not to read it, on account of the fact that it's addressed to my mom and not me. But seeing how I'm supposed to start acting like a detective and all, and part of being a detective is snooping, here's what the note says:

> *Dear Mrs. Crumb,*
> *Today was not the best day for Penelope.*
> *Once again, she was not paying attention*
> *in math. And, in the middle of my lesson*
> *on coats of arms, it came to my attention*
> *that Penelope had defaced Patsy Cline's*
> *drawing. This caused quite a disturbance*
> *as you can imagine. I can't for the life of*
> *me figure out why she would want to do*
> *that to a drawing of her own face. When I*
> *asked Penelope, she replied simply that her*

nose needed to be fixed. Maybe you can get
to the bottom of this?

Sincerely, Ms. Stunkel

There's a word in the note I don't know: *defaced*. It must have something to do with making a face look better. I stuff the note back in the envelope and stick it in my toolbox. Then I deliver it to Mom.

"Oh dear," Mom says, before she even reads it. She puts down her paintbrush. She's got a new batch of insides that she's working on.

I look them over real close and point to one of a purplish red blob. "What's that?"

"A spleen."

"Spleen?" I say. "That sounds made-up."

When Mom opens the letter, her face gets all pinched. "Penelope Rae." (Spleen.) "What is this about?"

"I defaced my face," I say.

"Do you know what *defaced* means?"

"Not exactly."

"It means to ruin something," Mom says.

"Ruin? That can't be right," I say. "Are you sure it doesn't mean to make a face look better?"

Mom shakes her head. "Sometimes you act like you were raised by wolves. What were you thinking?"

"I was thinking that Patsy Cline drew my nose, which is also Grandpa Felix's nose, all wrong."

"What does Felix have to do with this?" Mom says.

"It's *his* nose," I tell her.

Mom gives me a look that says, We Are Not Going to Talk about This Anymore. And then she says, "We are not going to talk about this anymore."

"If Grandpa Felix's nose isn't on my face, then it's like Grandpa Felix doesn't even exist." I start to feel all tingly in my fingers. "Like he's never been here." And if he's never been here, then Dad's never been here. But I keep that last part to myself.

She dips her paintbrush into a blob of deep red

and then sweeps the brush across her paper. "Some-times people aren't here for you when you need them to be."

"Dad isn't here for me when I need him to be."

Mom flinches when I say this like I stuck her with a pin. Sometimes I try to say things with sharp edges to get her talking. But it never works. "To your room," she says. "Oh, and you're going to tell Patsy Cline that you're sorry about what you did to her picture."

"But I'm not sorry," I say.

She gives me a look that says, Oh Yes, You Are, Young Lady.

"Okay, fine," I say. But I'm not going to mean it.

I stomp all the way to my room, where I find Littie digging headfirst in my closet. "Don't you have any hats?" she says.

"What for?"

Littie shakes a bag of marshmallows at me and sticks her head out from under my Captain Hook Halloween costume. "I'm making a marshmallow helmet." She pulls out my Hook hat. "Can I have this?"

"I guess." I was Captain Hook in first grade, and the hat is getting too small for my head. I climb onto my bed and pull my toolbox onto my lap. I turn the magnifying glass over in my hand and then hold it up to my eye.

"Do you have any of the big marshmallows?" Littie asks. "All we have are the miniatures."

I shake my head. "A helmet for what?"

"I'm going to learn how to ride a skateboard," she says. "And I need head protection in case I crash."

"Oh." Through the magnifying glass, I look at the bag she's holding. "They look like the big ones in here."

"What do you have that for?" she asks.

"We are supposed to be detectives for Miss Stunkel's class. Snoop around and dig up things about our family. Stuff like that."

"What kind of things?" Littie says.

I shrug. "Something good for my arm coat."

"What's an arm coat?" she says.

"I don't know," I tell her. "But if I make a good enough one, I'll be like Leonardo da Vinci."

Littie raises her eyebrows at me and then glues a marshmallow on my Hook hat. "Are you sure you don't have any of the big marshmallows?"

"Littie," I say, "I can't think about marshmallows now. I've got to be a detective and save all of my brains for my arm coat and family dirt-digging-up."

"Do you mean a coat of arms?" she asks.

"Maybe."

"Can I help?"

But I'm already down the hall when I answer. "I'm calling my nanny and pop-pop."

"I thought your grandparents were dead," says Littie, catching up.

"No," I say. "Not these ones."

7.

I pick up the phone and dial. "Hi, Aunt Renn, this is Penelope."

"Hi, Melon. What a nice surprise," she says. Aunt Renn is my mom's sister. She lives in Texas and has always called me Melon since I can remember. It has something to do with cantaloupes and my name being Penelope, but it never made any sense to me. That's my aunt Renn for you.

"Are Nanny and Pop-Pop home?"

"You just missed them," she says. "They piled into their RV and headed west to some flea market.

You can call them on their cell phone. Do you have the number?"

I tell her that I do, and then I say, "I'm doing a school project about our family history. Do you know anything?"

"Not much," she says. "What kind of stuff do you want to know?"

"Something good enough that I could put on an arm coat," I say. "Like, was anybody in our family famous?"

"I came in second place in a spelling bee in fifth grade," she says. "*Embarrassment*. That was the word I missed. E-M-B-A-R-A-S-S-M-E-N-T. I think that's it. I can never remember if it has two *r*'s or two *s*'s."

"Huh," I say and then nothing else.

"But your uncle Cleigh would know more about that than I do," she says. "About our family, I mean. He never was a very good speller."

"Uncle Cleigh?" I say, after punching in his number. "It's Penelope. Can you tell me something about our family that's not boring or about spelling?"

Uncle Cleigh says he's been studying about our family's genie-ology. Which sounds really good until he tells me that genie-ology doesn't have anything to do with magic genies. So, I hang up.

"Hi, Nanny."

"Penelope, sweetness. How are you?" she says. "Pop and I are at a flea market outside of Austin. We're about to buy a lamp."

"Do you know anything real good about our family?"

Nanny says, "I beg your pardon? What *isn't* good about our family? Answer me that." Then she says something else about a lamp shade and a new plug.

"Huh?"

"Oh, Penelope. We're talking lamps here. Can I ring you later?"

"Wait, before you go," I say. "Do you know if Grandpa Felix still lives in Simmons?"

"Felix?" says Nanny. "Lost track of that one years ago. Why do you ask?"

I tell her "no good reason" and then hang up.

Littie's got half of my Hook hat covered in marshmallows. "Your family is very dull," she says.

Maybe they are, but having a dull sort of family is the kind of thing you can't do anything about and don't really want to hear from somebody else. "What's so great about your family?" I say.

Littie shrugs and then, like she gets asked this very question all the time, she says, "My mom and dad are both scientists and worked in Africa on finding cures for diseases. My dad still does that, except not in Africa anymore, but my mom stopped working after I was born so she could concentrate on me. My grandpa on my mom's side was an astronaut and got to go into outer space. My grandma is a reporter and got to meet the president, but I don't remember which one. My other grandpa, the one with the spider legs, flies airplanes."

Well then. Nobody likes a big shot.

"I'm just saying," she says. "But don't feel bad. I'd trade you." She squints her eyes, shakes her finger, and says, "Because there are no adventures allowed," in a creaky, high-pitched voice that sounds a good bit like her momma's. Even looks like her, too.

"Sure," I say, even though I wouldn't trade families with Littie no matter what. Not even if they got a TV and her momma started letting her do stuff and quit putting ice cubes in milk.

"What about your dad's family?" says Littie. "I mean, they might be not as dull."

"My dad didn't have any brothers or sisters," I tell her.

"A Lonely Only like me?"

"Yep."

"What about his mom?" she asks.

"Dead," I say. "So, there's just his dad, Grandpa Felix. Now that he's not dead anymore."

Littie chews on a marshmallow. "The one with the nose?"

I nod.

"Do you think he'd be any better than the rest of your family?" She pauses. "And by the way, I wasn't looking at your nose just now. And even if I was looking at your nose, which I was *not*, it's not because it's big. I thought there was something on it."

"Fine." I pull the picture of Grandpa Felix from my pocket.

"Where did you get that?" Littie asks.

"From the photo album." I touch my finger to Grandpa Felix's nose in the picture and can just about see him wink at me.

"Did you have a hook with this costume?" asks Littie.

"What?"

"Captain Hook has a hook for a hand, you know," she says. "That's why they call him Captain Hook."

"In there somewhere." I point to the bottom of my closet without taking my eyeballs off Grandpa.

"Like a treasure hunt." She starts throwing things out of my closet. Shirts fly by my head—pink ones, the kind I don't like and never wear because pink makes me feel like a raw hot dog and at the same time a baby pig with a temperature. One shirt hits me in the face.

"Watch it," I say, pulling the shirt off my head.

"Found it!" Littie holds up the hook made out of aluminum foil wrapped around a coat hanger. "If only we could find some real buried treasure."

Now, I'm telling no lies when I say that I see Grandpa Felix just about give me another wink right then and there. So I say to Littie, "Maybe we can."

Littie's eyes get so big, her cheeks might fall in, and she says, "I smell an adventure." I grab my magnifying glass and we head for the computer.

"What are you doing, dorkus?" says Terrible. We run into him as he comes out of the kitchen.

I shrug at him and try to slip past, but he blocks me.

"Hey, we learned about noses in biology class today," he says.

He leans in close and my nose twitches at his bad smell. I switch to breathing through my mouth and look for other alien signs like scales and pointy teeth, but I don't see any.

"Noses never stop growing," he says, waiting for my reaction.

But I don't say anything and try to keep my face blank.

"Ears, too. Haven't you ever noticed how old people have giant noses and ears?"

Littie's eyes get big and she says, "I *have* noticed that! I'm just saying."

"See?" he says. "Even when the rest of them stop growing, their noses just keeping on getting bigger and bigger and bigger and . . ."

I hold the magnifying glass up to my eye and peer at him until his nose is the size of a baked potato. He rolls his eyes, mutters *weirdo* under his breath, and then lets me by. Aliens are not to be trusted (Number 2).

At our computer, I do a search for Felix Crumb. Apparently, there are a lot of Felix Crumbs out there. Too many. But none that actually live near

me. Still, it makes me wonder how many Penelope Crumbs there are. But when I ask Littie, she clucks her tongue like a pigeon and says, "Do you want to find your grandpa or not?" I tell her fine and that when she clucks her tongue I want to throw bread crumbs at her.

Littie looks at the screen over my shoulder and says, "Maybe you should hire a private detective. They find people all the time."

"*I* am a detective," I tell her. "And I've only just started finding people." I search for F. Crumb, instead of Felix, in Maryland.

Littie points at the computer. "It says there is one F. Crumb in Simmons and two F. Crumbs in Montville. They're not that far from here."

"Mom said Grandpa Felix used to live in Simmons," I say. "That's got to be him!" I print out the telephone numbers and addresses and fold the paper in half. "We used to go to Simmons a lot when Nanny and Pop-Pop lived there. Before they got their camper and went exploring." I stuff the paper under my shirt in case there is an alien inspection before I can get back to my toolbox.

"What are you going to do with those?" she asks.

"Littie Maple, we're going on a treasure hunt. Only this treasure is the not-buried kind."

8.

I take the phone to my bedroom, and Littie follows, poking the back of my head with the hook. We make it to my room without any alien encounters, thank lucky stars. And as soon as we get there, I pull out the paper from under my shirt and unfold it.

"Want me to call out the numbers while you dial?" asks Littie, pulling on the corner of the paper.

"No," I say, grabbing the paper with both hands. "I don't."

Littie lets go then and sticks out her bottom lip like I've stomped on her feelings. I try to explain that the names on the paper are like a secret code or a map or a key or something that will lead me to my grandpa, and that I want to do it myself. Which makes her bottom lip stick out even more.

"You can still help me," I tell her, "but just not for this first part."

Littie crosses her arms and lets out a "fine" with a huff blowing out of her mouth behind it. But I don't care so much because I'm about to talk to my grandpa. "Which one are you going to call first?" she says, looking at the ceiling. "If I'm allowed to ask a question."

I give her a look that says, Don't Be a Dork, and then I say, "The one in Simmons." My fingers start to shake a little as I dial the only F. Crumb in Simmons. I hold my breath, not sure what I'm going to say when Grandpa Felix answers. Littie pulls my arm toward her so we can both listen to the phone.

"First ring," she says. Her eyes get big, and I

match their size with mine. Littie reaches out her hook hand to me, and I squeeze it.

"Second ring," she says.

My heart moves into my ears, making them feel sweaty.

The rings keep coming, and Littie counts every one up to seven. At number eight, before Littie has a chance to get out a sound, I say, "Enough with the counting already, for Pete's sake."

Littie's face gets red and she pulls her hook out of my hand, but at least she's quiet and there's no reminder that there's no grandpa answering on the other end. Other than the fact that there's no grandpa answering on the other end.

"Maybe he's just away," Littie says.

"Of course he's away," I tell her. "That's usually what it means when somebody doesn't answer the phone."

"You don't have to be nasty about it," she says. "I just mean that he may be out on one of his adventures or something."

"Maybe." I hang up the phone. "But I thought he would at least have an answering machine. With a message that says, 'I wish I could talk to you, my darling, but I'm not here to answer the phone because I am on an important expedition to find the very rare painted lady butterfly. A challenging and most important task, indeed.'"

"That's what you think his answering machine would say?" Littie scratches her face with the hook.

"What's so wrong with that?" I say.

"For one thing, *butterflies?*"

I sift through the Heap, looking for matching socks. "I've been thinking about Grandpa Felix. And I've decided that he probably likes to go on nature walks, knows how to catch butterflies without tearing their wings, and is real good at fixing things."

"Fixing what kind of things?" asks Littie.

"Broken things. Things that aren't working like they should."

"You mean like your mom's dryer?"

"And other things, too." Bigger things.

"Oh," she says. And then after a while she blurts out, "Nature walks?"

I give her a look that says, What's Wrong with Nature Walks?

"Fine," Littie says. "Nature walks and butterflies. But I still don't think his answering machine message would say that."

"Why not?"

"Because everybody knows it's not a good idea to say you're not home on your answering machine when you're not home because robbers would know you're not home and could steal all your stuff. Including your television."

"Okay, Littie."

"But even if that *is* your grandpa's number, and even if he *is* on some painted lady butterfly hunt, how are you going to find him? I mean, he could be gone for a year. Or more even. I'm just saying."

Well then. The thing about Littie is that she thinks the worst a lot. And most of the time, the worst is not what I want to be thinking about. Especially when it comes to my grandpa. "There could be other reasons why he doesn't answer, you know."

"Like what?" Littie says. But before I can even get a word in, she says, "Like he could be tied up by robbers and can't reach the phone. Or he could have slipped and hit his head on the tub and now can't remember how to answer a phone. Or even remember what a phone is for!"

I give Littie a look that says, You Sound Just Like Your Momma. But Littie's not as good as me about telling what different faces mean, so she says, "What?"

I just shake my head and say "nothing," because if she doesn't know how much she's like her momma then I am not going to be the one to tell her. I fold up the paper with the addresses and phone numbers of the F. Crumbs on it, and I drop it into my toolbox.

"What about the F. Crumbs in Montville?" Littie asks.

"On second thought, I don't think the first words I say to my long-lost grandpa should be done on the phone. I think I'll go and see for myself in person."

"Face-to-face?" says Littie.

I nod. "Nose to nose."

9.

What are you up to?" asks Terrible the next morning in a way that makes me think he knows what I'm up to.

"Nothing." I let the granola bars, bologna sandwiches, and water bottles fall from my arms into my toolbox. I push aside the stack of dirty cereal bowls on the kitchen counter and grab two apples from the fruit basket. Terrible watches me as I drop the apples into my toolbox and latch it shut.

"It doesn't look like nothing."

I shrug and then finger the picture of Grandpa Felix in my pocket.

"I'm serious, dork," he says. "Mom is at school all day today, so I'm in charge. And you've got a list of Saturday chores to do."

Suddenly I'm Orphan Annie left with mean ole Miss Hannigan to scrub the floor until it shines like the top of the Chrysler Building. It's a hard-knock life having an alien for a brother. "I've already cleaned my room, and it's your turn to do the dishes," I say. The last part is true at least. "Littie and me are going to work on a school project."

Terrible gives me the Stink Eye, but I put on my best Don't Look at Me, I Didn't Kill the Canary face. His alien mind reading must be on the blink today, though, because after a staring contest that practically makes me go cross-eyed he leaves me alone.

The plan is to meet Littie downstairs, in front of our building. When I get there, she's hiding behind the trunk of the pear tree in my mini-marshmallowed Captain Hook hat.

"What do you have that on for?" I ask.

"Detectives wear hats. I needed a hat. Did you bring the magnifying glass?"

I pat my toolbox. "Got it. Do you have the tickets?"

She pulls two plastic metro cards from her shirt pocket and smiles. "One is mine from the last time we went to the aquarium. And I borrowed the other one," she says, biting her thumb. I raise my eyebrows. "What Mom doesn't know won't hurt her. I'm just saying. Did you get the provisions?"

"Huh?"

Littie slips the cards back into her pocket. "Food and stuff. You know, in case of emergency."

I nod and recite the long list of food I crammed in my toolbox. Which now weighs a ton. Littie grabs part of the metal handle to share the load. "I figure we should try the F. Crumb in Simmons first," I tell her. "Since he used to live there. And if that F. Crumb isn't the right F. Crumb, we'll try the ones in Montville."

"Good plan," says Littie. "Let's move." She tip-toes away from the tree.

I start tiptoeing, too. After a while I say, "Are we going to do this the whole way to the metro station? It's hard on the legs."

Littie stops and plants her heels. "I guess we could be the kind of detectives that don't tiptoe around." I tell her that my legs think that's a fine idea.

We make it to the metro station after stopping twice—once for snacks and water that we gobbled up while resting on somebody's porch stoop, and once when I get a pebble in my shoe that turns out to be an acorn. Littie talks nonstop the whole en-tire way there. About what, I'm not sure because my brains are thinking about what it will be like seeing Grandpa Felix.

Inside the metro station, it's dark and damp and smells like a wet towel that's been left in the Heap for too long. "Why do you suppose your grandpa hasn't talked to you all these years?" says Littie.

"What do you mean?"

"If he *is* one of these F. Crumbs, that means he's probably lived near you all this time. And unless it's like you say, that he's been on some big butterfly expedition or is fixing some top secret satellite for NASA or got lost on one of his nature walks, why wouldn't he come to see you? I mean, you're his family. It doesn't make sense."

That makes my chest burn. I don't have an answer, not a good one, anyway. So I say what my mom always says when I ask her Why questions. "The world sometimes doesn't make a lot of sense."

Littie shrugs. "I guess."

We're about to get on the escalator to go down into the tunnel when a thought sinks me. I stop walking and lose my grip on the toolbox handle.

"Hey," says Littie, grabbing the toolbox with both hands. "What's the matter? You don't look so good."

People push by us, almost run over us. Littie steers me off to the side. "Do you think," I say slowly, "that the reason Grandpa Felix stopped coming around after my dad died, the reason he hasn't seen us all these years, is because of his nose?"

"What are you talking about?"

"Terrible said that noses never stop growing, Littie. What if his nose is bigger than his face and he doesn't want anybody to see and wanted us to think he was dead. Do you think that's why?" I start to panic, because if that's what happened to Grandpa Felix, then that's what I'm in for. "What if people throw rocks at him and call him Nose Man or Rhinoceros or something terrible like that and he can't get a job or go to a restaurant except on Thanksgiving because hardly anybody goes to a restaurant on Thanksgiving. Do you think that's why, Littie? Do you?"

"If his nose is bigger than his face," says Littie, looking me square in the eye, "then he'd probably be in the *Guinness Book of World Records*. He'd be a celebrity and sign autographs at the mall. And probably people at NASA would want to examine him and pay him a million dollars if he donated his nose to science. Does that sound like a reason not to leave your house?"

I shake my head.

"Exactly," she says, pulling on my arm. And we step onto the escalator.

The metro is crowded, but we find two seats together in the second car from the end. The smell hits me as soon as we sit down. It's like the inside of Terrible's shoes. I look around. Me and Littie seem to be the only ones making a Hold Your Nose, It Stinks to High Heaven in Here face. Doesn't anybody else smell it?

For a second I worry that maybe Terrible has followed us. I look around and I hold my breath, because 1) I'm expecting to see Terrible's face at any second, and 2) it smells so bad I think I might upchuck. But there's no sign of Terrible anywhere, thank lucky stars.

Littie holds her nose with one hand and opens the map with the other. I switch to breathing from my mouth. "Five stops before we get to Simmons," she says.

I hug my toolbox to my chest and wish that I'd brought my drawing pad. So many people to draw. So many different shapes and sizes of noses. I try to find all of the big ones to compare to mine. I point to a lady sitting across the way from us. "Is my nose bigger than hers?"

Littie looks at us both and whispers, "Yep. And be more quiet about it, would you? I think she heard."

I give the lady a friendly Sorry about What I Said wave. Then I point to a man in a bow tie. "What about him? Is my nose bigger than his?" I ask softly.

Littie says, "Definitely. Now stop it with all the questions, would you, I need to look at the map."

While Littie studies the map and rambles on about shortcuts and street names, I turn around to get a load of all the noses behind me. A man in the seat right behind me is leaning his head on the window. He has wrinkled skin that drapes over his bones like a tablecloth. His eyes are shut and his mouth is open so far that I can count twelve teeth on the bottom and eight up top.

He is very still. And after a while I think maybe too still.

I turn back around and shove my toolbox onto Littie's lap. "What *are* you doing?" she snaps, folding up the map.

I shush her and then face backward again, sliding up on my knees. I stare at the man for a long time until I'm sure he must be mostly dead. Maybe even all dead. His eyes stay closed during each stop, even when the name of the next station blares from the loudspeaker and the doors fly open and shut like elevators in a mood. The man doesn't move, not even a twitch. I reach out my finger.

"Penelope, no . . . ," says Littie.

My finger gets closer and closer to his face. The *whir* of the train is loud in my ears. The windows go black. And I pretend that we are speeding through time so fast, so far, that we're chasing the night and leaving the day in the dust. There's no telling where we will end up. There's no telling what can happen.

I hold tight to the back of the seat with my free hand as the train rocks and jolts. I can feel Littie's eyes on me. My eyes, though, are fixed on the space between the dead man and my finger. And the smaller that space gets, the more goose pimples I get on my arms.

The train jolts again, and before I'm ready the space is gone. The tip of my finger hits the tip of the dead man's nose. Right away, his eyes fly open. Which practically scares the life out of me. But somehow, with him alive and me now almost dead, my finger stays put on his nose.

We both stare at my finger. We're quiet, watching. Me, scared to take my finger away in case he might go dead again. Him, looking at my finger all cross-eyed like it is a butterfly on a blade of grass that might fly away at any second. As the train screeches to a stop, my finger slips to the side of his nose, but I manage to slide it back up again. His eyes are fixed on it.

"Come on, Penelope," says Littie, yanking at my arm and causing my finger to break away. "We need to get off."

I grab the handle of my toolbox as she pulls me off the metro. Over my shoulder, I look back at the man. He looks at me for a second, not even a second really, and as the doors close, so do his eyes. And then he is gone.

10.

When we get to Highland Street, the street where the only F. Crumb in Simmons lives, my heart is pounding. I pull at the neck of my T-shirt and have a look down at my chest. I imagine the insides heart that my mom drew pumping away inside me. And thinking about all the blood and veins and creepy stuff like that makes it pound even harder.

"Shush," I tell it, first in a firm voice like how you would tell a dog to stay, and then again much softer like when you find out that dog would rather not be told what to do.

"There it is!" says Littie, pointing. Which just about stops my heart altogether.

We stop in front of a yellow row house with pink shutters and a small garden in the front.

"Well, if your grandpa likes nature walks, he might just live in a place like this," says Littie. She pulls a leaf off a tall plant that's sticking up through the fence and brings it to her nose. "Peppermint."

She hands the leaf to me, and after I smell it, I slide the leaf carefully into my pocket. Then I open the white iron gate and pull Littie along the stone walkway and up the three steps to the front door.

My heart is beating so fast, I think it might jump right out and flop onto the ground next to my feet. Which wouldn't be the best way to meet your grandpa for the first time.

I practice what I'm going to say in my head. *Mr. Crumb, my dead dad is your son. Which makes you my grandpa. Can I call you Grandpa? Pappy? Pop? My, Grandpa, what a big nose you have.*

"Are we going to stand out here all day?" asks Littie. "Aren't you going to knock? Want me to do it? I'm just saying."

Good gravy. I raise my hand, hold my breath, and tap on the door. Littie takes a tiny step back and gives me a look that says, I Can't Believe We're Doing This. My heart is beating faster and I feel sick and woozy. Which makes me afraid because what if I go dead for real. Right now in front of Grandpa Felix. And then he'll have a dead son and a dead granddaughter. "I can't," I say to no one in particular. This was a bad idea. I turn to run.

But before my feet can figure out what they are supposed to do, I hear the door open.

I turn my head just to get a quick look at him, but there's no grandpa standing in the doorway. A woman in a bathrobe leans down toward us. That's when I see the cat curled up in her arms.

"Making repairs?" the woman asks.

"Huh?" I say, staring at the cat's belly to see if it's breathing.

"Looks like you've got your tools," she says, nodding at my toolbox.

"Oh, right," Littie says. "Tools." Then she gives me a look that says, I Hope She Isn't Counting on Us to Fix Anything.

Unless bologna sandwiches and half-eaten granola bars can fix what she's got broke, we aren't going to be much help. "Do you live here all by yourself?" I say.

My heart starts to pound again while I wait for her answer. I try to peer around her and have a look inside the door to see if maybe Grandpa Felix is just past her, there sitting at his desk putting a check mark beside his latest catch in *The National Audubon Society Field Guide to North American Butterflies*.

"No," she says, pushing her thick glasses to the top of her nose and standing up straight. "Not all by myself. It's me and the mister."

I knew it. Grandpa lives here. I peer around her again and point inside. "It looks like your table leg

in there is loose." I push past her, pulling Littie and my toolbox along with me and into the house.

"Now, wait a second," says the woman.

"What are you doing?" whispers Littie.

But I'm too busy looking for any sign of Grandpa Felix to answer. "Is he here?"

"Is who here?" says the woman.

"Your mister," I say.

The woman laughs, holds out her cat to me, and says, "Right in front of your nose, dear." The cat opens one eye, sees Littie's marshmallowed hat, and meows. "This is Mr. Jiggs."

"Aww," says Littie, reaching for the cat. "Can I hold him?"

The woman shakes her head. "I just got him back after he went wandering the city for a few days, so his nerves are shaken, if you don't mind. My nerves, too. I put up posters around the neighborhood and everything. Lucky he had the sense to find his way back home."

"Then *you're* F. Crumb?" I say.

"Francesca," says the woman. "Now, which table?"

I grab Littie's hand and pull her toward the door. "Your table leg looks fine then," I say on the way out. "My mistake."

Back on the metro, we're speeding toward Montville. This train doesn't stink near as bad as the other one, thank lucky stars, but it's so crowded, we can't get a seat. "It's only five stops," says Littie when I set the toolbox on the floor between my feet and lean my head against the metal pole by the doors.

I don't so much care about having to stand. My brains are fixed on finding the real F. Crumb: explorer, handyman, insect-lover, long-lost grandpa, and who knows what else. The train rattles and shakes, and we're so deep underground that my ears close up. The train conductor says something that sounds like "Nah fopp bonkpill" over the loudspeaker. "What did he say?" I ask Littie.

Only I must have said it real loud because two

people standing on the other side of Littie say to me, "Next stop Montville."

Littie rolls her eyes at me like she's never had plugged-up ears before, and then she squeezes her nose. I sniff the air but can't smell anything that's so bad, so I figure it must be coming from those two people beside Littie. I pick up my toolbox, thank the people for being so helpful and not rolling their eyes at me like Littie did, and tell them that I don't think they stink at all. Then I explain that we're off to find my grandpa. They say something else that I can't hear, but is probably something like "good luck" or "I hope you find him." Because that's what helpful people on a train would say.

We ride an escalator up and out of the metro station, and when we reach the street my ears finally get unplugged. "You were really loud in there," says Littie, reaching for my toolbox.

"At least I didn't make those people feel bad about the way they smelled," I say, shifting the toolbox to my other side.

"What do you mean?"

"The way you held your nose," I say.

Littie rolls her eyes at me again. "I was trying to get my ears to open." She holds her nose again to show me. "You squeeze your nose and then blow."

"Where'd you learn that?"

"My grandpa, the one who's a pilot, showed me."

I don't know why, but that makes me tighten my grip on the toolbox and say, "Well, Littie Maple, aren't you just the luckiest girl on the planet to have a grandpa to show you those kinds of things."

Littie bites her thumbnail for at least two blocks after that. We don't say anything and I'm not even sure where we're going because Littie is the one with the map. Finally, she stops biting and walking and says, "There."

A sign that says GOOD TO THE LAST CRUMB BAKERY blinks in the window in front of us. "Here?" I say. "But this can't be . . ."

"Come on," says Littie. "We might as well see. And I could use a cupcake."

I follow Littie inside right up to the counter. She orders a red cupcake with white frosting from the man at the register, and she lets out a squeal when he puts it in her hand. "Do you use beets in your red velvet?"

"Beets? I don't think so."

"Really?" she says. "I guess that's gone out of fashion. Many bakers used beets during World War Two to color their cakes. You know, because food was in short supply . . ."

I don't know why she's talking about beets when we're supposed to be detectives on a case, so I elbow her in the side so she'll remember why we're here. It works, because then she says, "Excuse me, sir. Can you tell me if a Mr. Felix Crumb is the proprietor of this business?"

Where Littie learned to talk like that I don't know. The man wipes his hands on his apron and says, "No, Frederick Crumb owns the place. He's in the back with the croissants. Do you want to chat him up about beets?"

I tell the man, "No, thank you, we definitely do not," and then we leave.

Once outside, I pull the paper with the F. Crumb addresses on it from my pocket. The peppermint leaf from Francesca's garden falls to the ground and I just leave it there. I cross off the two F. Crumbs and stare at the address of the only one left on the list: 247 East Montgomery Avenue.

Littie hands me half of her cupcake and says, "Let's go. Third time's the charm."

There's no charm at 247 East Montgomery Avenue. Which is exactly what I tell Littie when we get to the lobby of the apartment building and see the names of the people who live there posted just inside the door. F. Crumb at 247 East Montgomery Avenue is actually Fern P. Crumb. Fern, like the plant. Not Felix, like the grandpa.

The walk back to the Montville metro station is long, and I wish I had never eaten half of Littie's red cupcake because, beets or no beets, it's not agreeing with me. Littie tries her best to cheer me up on the way, saying things like, "At least we had an adventure" and "Your grandpa will turn up someday." Which doesn't make me feel one bit better.

"Look!" says Littie, pointing to a line of trash cans outside the metro station. "Did you see that cat?"

I don't see anything but garbage. "Mr. Jiggs probably escaped again."

"No, this one's gray," she says. "Aww! I wonder who he belongs to."

I shrug. "I hope he can find his way back home." And then I don't know how it comes into my brains, but that runaway cat makes me think of a way to help Grandpa Felix find his way home to us.

11.

There don't seem to be any dead people, or even mostly dead people, on the metro on our way home, thank lucky stars, so I keep my finger to myself.

The whole way Littie is talking up our adventure like we just sailed around the world on a raft made of peacock feathers. "We did it," she says with a smile on her face. "A real adventure. On our very own. And we didn't get lost or murdered or robbed or killed or kidnapped like my mom is always saying will happen."

"You're going with me tomorrow, right?" I say, as we climb the stairs of our apartment building. "To put up posters."

"Count me in," says Littie. "Are we going back to Montville? Because those cupcakes were good. I'm just saying."

"No, just Simmons. That's where Grandpa Felix used to live. Somebody should know him from the posters." In front of Littie's door I look her square in the eyeballs and say, "You can't tell a soul about our adventure, Littie. Cross your heart and hope to die a painful death."

"M-U-M is the word," she says, crossing her heart and her lips and then spitting on the floor to seal it.

But I don't know what M-U-M means or has to do with telling secrets. So I say, "Your M-U-M can't find out where we've been. Detectives have to be secret keepers."

We shake on it, but truth be told, it's really me that I'm worried about. Secret keeping is not my best subject.

As I take a step inside our apartment, every part of me tingles with secret knowing and I'm afraid that even my fingernails could give me away. But before I can even close the door behind me, Terrible is there with arms folded across his chest. Don't aliens have other things to do? I set down my toolbox by the door and try not to look at him.

"Where were you all day?" he asks.

It's best not to open my mouth in case my secret decides it wants to fly out, so I walk past him into the kitchen and pretend he's talking to somebody else. "Where's Mom?" I ask. If she's home, the chances of me being alien-murdered are pretty low, I figure.

"She's still at school." He follows me into the kitchen and corners me by the oven. He steps closer and the smell of him makes me cough. "Where were you?" he asks again.

"Littie's?" It comes out like a question.

"Try again," says the alien, "because Littie's momma came over here looking for you."

"Uh-oh."

"Uh-oh," Terrible repeated, leaning his face close.

I switch to breathing through my mouth. "Wha-wha-what did you tell her?"

His eyes lock on to me like they are trying to shoot out laser beams that will slice my brains in half (Number 10). "Wha-wha-what did I tell her? I told her that I didn't know where you were."

"But I said we were working on a school project!"

"You did?" he says. "I must have forgot."

"Terrible! Littie is going to be in big trouble with her momma now!"

"Calm down. First I told her that I didn't know where you were. But then I might have said something about a school project or something. When she started to get all worked up." He finally looks away from me like he decided that he couldn't kill me with laser beams. Which makes me wonder if my real brother is somewhere in there after all.

"You did?" I say.

His eyes are on me again. "That doesn't mean

I'm not going to tell Mom. Unless you say what you're up to."

I swallow. "A project for school is what I said we were doing, and that is what we did." I inch along the counter and keep going. "But we went outside for a while . . . outside . . . outside . . . outside because Littie wants to learn how to ride a skateboard. Right, and then she needed more marshmallows for her helmet, so we walked over to Muellers Drug Store. And you wouldn't think that would take all day, but those marshmallows take a long time to glue on. You know, because they are the mini kind. And it really did take a long time. And there might have been other things that we did, but those are the big parts."

Terrible leans in real close and stares at me, at my nose. "What are you looking at?" I ask, leaning backward against the counter.

"I'm just watching to see if your nose is growing with all the lies coming out of your mouth."

I cover my nose with my hand. The door to our

apartment opens and closes then, and Mom's voice calls out, "I'm home!"

"In here," says Terrible, giving me the Stink Eye.

"You won't really tell, will you?" I say.

Mom pops her head into the kitchen and smiles at us. "Had a great study session today. Let me just drop my books in the laundry and I'll make us dinner. How do ham-and-egg sandwiches sound?"

Terrible says "fine" and then puts his hand on my shoulder and squeezes. "Fine" comes out of my mouth before I know it and for a second I feel like a puppet. Pinocchio.

"I want to hear all about your day," says Mom as she heads down the hall.

"Did you hear that?" Terrible says, after she's gone. "She wants to hear all about your day." He smiles and gives my shoulder another squeeze. "Don't worry, I won't tell Mom what you've been up to today." I wait for the part that's going to sting. But I don't have to wait long. "All you have to do is give me your allowance."

"No." Aliens find sneaky ways to get your money (Number 9).

"Have it your way," he says. "Mother?"

"I'll be there in a second," she calls back.

Terrible grins at me, and I glare at him. Today it's my allowance, tomorrow he'll be stuffing my face into his sneakers. Mom's footsteps in the hallway get louder, closer. "Last chance," he says.

And only because I haven't found Grandpa Felix yet, I say fine.

12.

ater, after Mom goes to bed, I make copies of Grandpa Felix's picture on our printer and get to work on the posters. This is how they turn out:

Even though I gave Terrible all of my allowance and don't have any money left for a reward, I decide that a reward can be lots of things and doesn't have to mean only money. For example, I could draw a picture, make a ham-and-egg sandwich, or even show them a real live alien.

Mom has already left for somewhere by the time I get up. Before I can think of a way to leave the apartment without getting caught by Terrible, Littie Maple comes knocking. She's got a look on her face that says, I'm Not Supposed to Be Here.

She holds up the stopwatch she's got in her hand. "I've got exactly four minutes and twenty-eight seconds to tell you what I have to tell you before my momma gets out of the shower. So don't say anything."

"Okay," I say.

"Don't even say okay. There's no time for okay."

I nod and wonder if there's even time for that.

Littie takes a deep breath and says, "I got in a large amount of trouble yesterday because I was gone so long and didn't check in like I'm supposed to, and now I'm not allowed to leave Momma's sights. So . . ."

"But today we're supposed to . . ."

Littie puts her hand over my mouth and says, "Sorry, but I can't go with you to put up posters today." She cocks her head like she heard something. "I better go. But don't worry, I didn't tell Momma where we went or anything or that I was even with you the whole time, so I don't think she'll say anything to your mom. I'm just saying." Then she's gone before I can say anything else.

All of a sudden, I'm Sherlock Holmes without a Watson. A detective without an assistant is like a foot without toes. What I need is another Watson. So I call up Patsy Cline Roberta Watson and pull at my shoestrings until she answers.

"Mom wants to know if we're picking you up or you're meeting us there," she says without even saying hello.

I have no idea what she is talking about and

wonder if she thinks she's talking to someone else. So I say, "This is Penelope Crumb calling."

"I know who it is I'm talking to," she says, jabbing her words at me like they are made of spears.

"Oh," I say, "in that case, meet you where?"

"The All-Star Kids auditions. You didn't forget, did you?"

I pull the phone away from my ear because the spears are sharper now. Truth be told, I kind of did forget on account of the fact that my brains have been busy with other important things. For example, finding my grandpa Felix and trying not to get alien-murdered. Both things take up a lot of brain space and must have squeezed out the tiny little pea-size thing about going with Patsy Cline to the All-Star Kids auditions today.

But this is not what I tell Patsy Cline because that is not the sort of thing you say to your best friend. So I say, "Of course I didn't forget. But here's the thing . . ."

"Oh, whew!" says Patsy. "For a second there

I thought you were going to say you forgot all about my audition and aren't coming. I mean, that would be worse than dropping a glazed doughnut in a sandbox. Especially after the nose incident at school."

And that's when I decide not to say anything about putting up posters to find my long-lost grandpa. Instead I make up a teeny, tiny white lie about how my mom is sick with a mysterious flu bug and needs me to stay here and bring her beef bouillon cubes in hot water. Which is the only thing that will keep her from going dead.

"What kind of flu bug?" she asks. "Can you catch it?" Patsy Cline has a thing about germs ever since the time we learned that some germs have tails.

"I think it's one of those alien bugs," I whisper.

Patsy Cline seems very worried after I tell her this and says, "Don't think a thing about All-Star Kids. You have to stay home with your mom, Penelope. So she can get better lickety-split."

I tell her that I know she will. And after I hang up, a strange thing happens. My nose does some twitching. I put my hand over my nose to make sure it didn't grow any just now. Then I say out loud, "It's not like Patsy Cline needs me there at the auditions with her or anything. She's sung without me plenty of times. Besides, she's got her mom. Which means she's not all by herself like me."

I pack up my toolbox, roll up my posters, and tell Terrible that I'm going to the library. I tell him this while he's in the bathroom, while the water's running. And I say it in a whisper from the kitchen.

It's not my fault if he doesn't hear me.

After three blocks, I slow down a little and stop looking behind me for Terrible. I pat my shirt pocket to make sure I still have Littie's metro card. Which I forgot to give back to her yesterday, thank lucky stars. Going on the metro is a little scary without Littie, but detectives have to be brave, especially when they are without their assistants.

Outside of the Simmons metro station I get out

my scissors and tape from my toolbox and fix a couple of posters to telephone poles. Then I head toward the neighborhood where I think Francesca and Mr. Jiggs live. Along the way, I put up more posters: on street signs, parking meters, and lamp-posts. But when I tape a poster to the side of a big mailbox in front of the Simmons post office, I find trouble.

"Just what do you think you're doing, girlie?" says a man with long sideburns that point like arrows to his mouth.

"Looking for someone," I say, pressing the tape on the corner of the poster.

"Look, you can't put that there," he says. "You're going to have to take that off right now."

"How come?"

"This here mailbox is government property," he says, "and you ain't allowed to put stuff on it."

"Says who?" I say. "There's no sign that says no posters allowed."

"Says me," he says. "I work here, so I should know something about it."

"You work here?" I say. "You're a mailman?"

"Not today, I'm not. It's Sunday." He nods at my poster. "You gonna take that off of there or what?"

I pull at the tape on the top of the poster. "Hey, if you're a mailman, I bet you know the names of all kinds of people in town."

"Some," he says.

"Did you ever deliver mail to a Felix Crumb?"

"Nope."

"Now, you answered way too fast. Why don't you think about it for a minute?" I hold the poster right in front of his face. "Felix Crumb, and here's what he looks like. Only his nose might be a little bigger now."

The man pushes the poster away. "I *said* nope."

Well then. I roll up the poster and shove it under my armpit. After he drops some letters into the mailbox, I follow him down the street. I keep close so I don't lose him if he decides to make a sharp turn down an alley or dive into a manhole. But all of a sudden when my eyeballs wander over to a giant sock monkey in the window of a toy store, the man stops to tie his shoelaces. And I run right into the back of him, dropping my poster.

"Are you still *here?*" he says.

"Yep." I pick up my poster. "Do you want to see his picture again?"

"Girlie, don't you have something better to do than trail me?"

"Nope," I say.

He sighs. "What's the name you're looking for again?"

"Felix Crumb." I say it slow so that it has a chance to really sink into his brains.

"And what makes you think he lives around here?" he asks.

"Because my mom said he used to."

"When?"

I shrug. "The other day."

He gives me a big eyeball roll. "I mean, when did he live here?"

"Oh, right. A long time ago."

"And you don't know where."

"No," I say.

"No address?"

"No."

"No phone number?"

"No."

"Girlie, a whole lot of nothing is what you have," he says, shaking his head. "Why do you want to find him?"

"Because he's my grandpa," I say.

The man scratches the pointy part of his sideburn. "How can you be so sure that this grandpa of yours wants to be found?"

"Because I am," I tell him. "He's a great adventurer, and . . . and . . ."

"And what?"

"And he just doesn't know I'm looking for him is all. If he knew, he'd try to find me, too."

The man rests on his knees and leans in close. He smells like bacon and cigarettes. "Tell you what. You leave me alone, and if I see a letter with Felix Crumb's name on it, I'll give you a call. Deal?"

I stick my hand out for shaking. "Deal."

13.

Somehow I know I'm in trouble even before I open the door to our apartment.

"Where in blazes have you been?" says Mom. She's standing next to Terrible, who looks proud like he just invented cotton candy or started a war. I can't tell which.

The secret tucked inside me feels heavy and wants to come out. I put my hand over my chest to keep it in. Then I search my brains about where I said I was going today, but it doesn't much matter because Mom has a lot more to say. "And be very careful about your answer because apparently I have a serious case of the flu and could take a turn for the worse at any moment."

"Patsy Cline," I say. I hadn't counted on this happening.

"Her mother, actually."

"Oh." Ten times worse.

"Imagine my surprise when I learned how sick I am."

"You are looking much better," I say.

"Penelope." (Diseased Stomach.) Mom folds her arms across her chest. "And how you had to miss Patsy's audition to stay home and take care of me."

It's hard to look at my mom when she's angry. Her eyes, nose, and mouth get all scrunched up together in the middle of her face like they're telling ghost stories at a tea party. I look at Terrible, which is a big mistake because he's pinching his nose with his fingers in a way that says I'm Pinocchio.

"Well," says Mom. "I'm waiting."

My secret starts knocking.

"Where were you today, missy?"

I know from experience it's best to give up, especially when she calls me *missy*. Which makes me glad that I've got the name Penelope for most of the time.

Finally, I blurt out, "I went looking for Grandpa Felix."

Not one single balloon or streamer falls from the ceiling. No confetti and no horns. Terrible goes all quiet, and Mom's face gets blotchy.

"I haven't found him yet," I say. "But I know I will soon."

Terrible is looking at me like I just opened a casket and out fell a dead body. "What?" I say. But he just shakes his head and then looks away.

Mom picks up her sketch pad of insides drawings from the coffee table and shuffles through the pages, like she's telling them what she's thinking. Things she doesn't tell us. Then she looks right at me. "Penelope, I want you to pay attention to what I'm about to say."

I set my eyeballs on her scrunched-up tea-party face.

"Felix Crumb is not a part of our life anymore," she says.

"But that's why I'm trying to find him," I say. "So he can be."

Mom shakes her head. "No. Don't you understand?"

I don't. Not even a little. And I don't think Grandpa Felix would understand this either. Even with my secret out, my chest feels heavy again. But I nod anyway and then cover my nose with my hand, just in case.

I make up a speech for Patsy Cline in my brains on the walk to school that says how very sorry I am. But when I see Patsy Cline in Miss Stunkel's classroom, she acts like I've got tails sprouting out all over.

"Patsy Cline Roberta Watson," I say, "you are my only best friend and I am sorry you're mad at me. I'm sorry for erasing my nose in the drawing that you did of me, even though the nose you drew didn't look anything like mine. And I'm sorry for drawing my nose over again, even though I made it look how my nose really does look even bigger-sized. And I'm also sorry for telling you that my mom was sick and almost dead so that I didn't have to go hear you sing."

When I'm done, Patsy Cline blinks her eyes about a million times like she's having an allergic reaction. And when she starts to turn away and doesn't say, "I could never stay mad at you, Penelope Crumb," I grab her arm and tell her that she can come over after school and sing like she did at her audition so it will be just like I was there.

Only, Patsy Cline says no and then nothing else.

The bell rings then, and Miss Stunkel says, "I'm allowing you some time today to work on your coat of arms. Not only will the winner's coat of arms be on display at the Portwaller-in-Bloom Spring Festival, but the winner will have a chance to make a speech and explain his or her work."

Angus Meeker raises his hand. "Can we do two coats of arms if we want?"

I look at him and roll my eyes. I'm an excellent eye roller.

"These are due on Friday, Angus," she says. "But I suppose, if you're that ambitious."

Angus Meeker says, "Ambitious," and then smiles at me, who knows what for. Then he pulls out a poster board from his desk and unrolls it. His coat of arms is in the shape of a shield made up of different colors of felt. And he's got glitter and pictures of all kinds of things on it.

Patsy Cline's got a purple cowboy hat on her coat of arms along with some music notes.

Miss Stunkel says, "Penelope, you're supposed to be working. This is no time for wandering eyes."

I take out my drawing pad and stare at an empty page. I shut my eyeballs tight and try to think about my family and what to put on my coat of arms, but all I can see is what's not there. And I know that drawing pictures of what used to be won't bring them back.

"Poor dear Penelope," Mister Leonardo da Vinci would say. "She knows nothing of her family, and therefore, she sits alone in the dark. An artist cannot draw in the dark, after all. No, an artist must have light to see."

"I'm trying to turn on the light," I whisper to Leonardo. "But I can't find him."

14.

Littie Maple has got something to say. She's waiting for me in our living room when I get home from school with a face that says, This Is Important. She follows me into my room, and as soon as my door is closed, she spills it. "I've been asking Momma for months if I could go to the Homeschooler's Craft Fair they have at the library on Tuesdays."

I nod and try to pretend like I know what she's talking about.

"And she's finally letting me go!" Littie's practically shaking when she says this, and her smile is so big, it could sprout legs and walk off.

I fall face-first on my bed because Littie might as well be talking upside down and backward about her grandpa's nose hairs. She sits on my legs and says, "Tomorrow is Tuesday. And Momma is going to drop me off at the library BY MYSELF for the whole day."

"So?" I say into my pillow.

"Your brain is as thick as mud." She pulls at my hair. "So, we can go on another adventure tomorrow."

"I have school," I remind her. "And besides, I'm all out of adventures."

"Well, I'm not," she says. "My adventures are just getting going." Littie gets up and opens the door. "Real detectives don't give up on a case, you know. I'm just saying."

I pull my pillow over my head to shut out all the light.

A long while later, when Littie's gone and the

apartment is quiet, I take the picture of Grandpa Felix and my dad out of my toolbox and return it to the family album. The faces in the pictures ask, "What are you doing up so late? A girl your age should be in bed by now." But I tell them all to be quiet and turn the pages quick.

When I slide the book back onto the shelf, a thin piece of paper sticks out of one of the pages. It's a page torn out of a magazine, and when I unfold it, a dog's face stares back at me. The dog gets my attention right away, but not because he looks more like a cow than a dog on account of the fact that he has brown and black spots all over his face. This dog has got one thing that makes me stop: bushy eyebrows. (Not the kind that are all caterpillary like Patsy Cline's Marge, but eyebrows all the same.)

If ever I was sure about a look on a face, it would be this one. This dog, who I've decided should be called Winston, is gazing off to the side somewhere, like he just heard somebody say, *Winston, come here, boy! It's time to play Chinese checkers!* Because that's what dogs with eyebrows do in their spare time.

When I look across the page to see who might be calling him, I see a name typed sideways along the picture in tiny letters that only mice could read: Mortimer Felix Crumb.

"Mortimer?" I say out loud. "Who's Mortimer?" Winston looks back at me as if he might just know the answer. "Could Grandpa Felix also be a Mortimer?" Winston won't say for sure, but his eyebrows tell me that if he could get out of that magazine page, he might be able to help track him down.

I fold up the page, take back the picture of Grandpa Felix and my dad, and decide to be a detective once more.

Terrible has got his alien eyeballs on me all morning. I take ant-size bites of my peanut butter toast and chew without making any noise and hope he

won't notice me. "What's going on?" he says, leaning across the table at me.

I shrug and say, "Nothing."

He pokes his finger into my shoulder. "It better be nothing."

"Ow. You can only do that because Mom is at work." Then I shove the rest of the toast into my mouth and rub my arm.

"Wish I had a sister who was at least half normal," he says, shaking his head. Like he's so normal or regular. He pokes my shoulder again, and this time it hurts so much that a piece of chewed-up toast falls out of my mouth.

I'm out the door with my toolbox and jacket before I can swallow the toast all the way down. Instead of going left on Washington Street to school, I go right and walk eight blocks to the library.

The Portwaller Public Library is full of homeschoolers. I find Littie off by herself, reading a book called *Everything You Need to Know about Skateboarding*. "Ready for an adventure?" I say.

Littie stuffs the book into her backpack and says, "What took you so long?" like she knew I was coming.

I take out the magazine page of Winston and point to Grandpa Felix's possibly new name. I tell Littie about how Grandpa Felix may also be Mortimer.

"Mortimer?" she says. "I guess if I had a name like that, I'd go by Felix, too."

"We need to do another search." At a library computer, we type in "Mortimer Crumb" and to my surprise we find one M. Crumb in Portwaller.

"He lives in the same town as we do!" says Littie.

I shake my head. "That can't be right. Why wouldn't he see us if he lived that close? Maybe that's not the right M. Crumb." But I write down his number and address just in case.

Littie says, "Come on, let's find out," and she leads me to the information desk where there's a phone on the counter.

"May I help you?" asks the man behind the desk.

"We need to make a local call," Littie tells him.

"Two, actually," I say.

"Two?" Littie whispers. I nod, and she tells the man, "That's right, two calls."

The man puts his hand on the phone and looks us over like he's trying to decide if we're bad eggs. Then Littie puts her arm around my shoulder and says, "Don't worry, I'm homeschooled. I mean, we both are. Homeschooled."

The man must decide that we aren't bad eggs because he takes his hand off the phone and says, "Make it short."

As Littie reads off the phone number, I dial and wait. Halfway through the first ring, I notice the man eyeballing us, so I give him a quick smile and then turn my back to him. Three rings later, a man with a gruff voice says, "What is it?" on the other end of the phone. Not *hello*, not *good morning*, not *Crumb residence, Mr. Mortimer Felix speaking. How can I help you?* This man says, "What is it?" like the sound of the ring grumped him up. And right away I know this man is my grandpa.

"Hi. Is this Mr. Crumb?"

"You called me," the man says. "Shouldn't you know who you called?"

Good gravy. "There are more than one or two Crumbs out there," I say. "So I want to be sure I've got the right one. Are you Mr. Mortimer Felix Crumb?"

"Depends on who's asking," he barks. "I don't give to charities, if that's what you're after. You sound too young to be asking for money. How old are you?"

"I'm nine. Going on ten."

"Is it him?" Littie whispers.

I whisper back, "I think so."

"Who else are you talking to?" he asks.

"Nobody."

"I distinctly heard you say 'I think so,' so don't lie to me and say you didn't," he says. "I may be up in years, but my wits and hearing are front and center and I don't like to be taken advantage of by shysters calling me up and looking for money."

I give Littie a face that says, I Think He Might Have Been Raised by Wolves.

"You've got five seconds to state your business, missy, or I'm hanging up."

"He called me 'missy,'" I whisper to Littie.

"I heard that."

"Oh," I say. "Sorry."

"Are you one of those prank callers?"

"No. This is no prank."

"Then what are you selling?" he says.

"What am I selling?" I repeat. I cover the phone with my hand and say to Littie, "He thinks I'm selling something."

She scratches her head. "Tell him you're selling marshmallows. No, wait. Tell him you're selling vacuum cleaners." I shake my head. "No, wait. Life insurance," she says.

The man on the phone is counting down fast. "Three . . . two . . ."

So I blurt out, without really thinking, "Do you have a dead son named Theodore Crumb because if you do, I am your granddaughter. I'm Penelope Rae . . ."

And before I can even say Crumb, that man, that Grandpa Felix, hangs up on me.

15.

That was him," I say, after telling Littie all the parts of our conversation that she didn't hear. "That was Grandpa Felix, or Mortimer, I mean, that I just talked to." My nose tingles and all of a sudden I feel like my heart doubled in size.

"How do you know for sure?" she says.

"I just do." Then I put my hands on Littie's shoulders and look her square in the eyeballs. "I need you to do me a favor and call my school and pretend you're my mom."

Littie raises her eyebrows at me and then looks

at the man behind the information desk. After a moment, she whispers, "What do you want me to say?"

I tell her to say that I'm sick with a very scary and contagious flu bug and won't be coming to school. "It's not flu season," she says.

I roll my eyes at her. "Then just say that it's not the flu but just some terrible disease that only lasts a day."

"What are your symptoms?" she says. "In case they ask."

"Nose and eyes that are stuffed full of green snot. A cough. Upchucking. And the runs. Fever of two hundred and five. Red bumps on my arms and cheeks. What's the thing called when you can't talk?"

"Laryngitis?"

"Yeah, that. And itching. Lots and lots of itching."

Littie says, "But I don't sound anything like your mom."

And then I come up with the very smart idea

that she should hold her nose while she talks and say that she's got the flu bug, too.

While Littie calls Portwaller Elementary, I talk to the man at the information desk to get some information. After I show him Grandpa Felix's address and ask how we can get there, he hands me a map and points to the bus stop in front of the library. "Next bus should be here in about three minutes."

I turn to Littie, who is still on the phone, holding her nose and saying, "I'm sure Penelope will be feeling much more chipper tomorrow, thank you ever so kindly." Which is something my mom would never ever say.

I pull at Littie's arm. "Come on, we have to go."

Littie hangs up quick, and I pull at her arm until we're both running out the front door toward the bus stop.

"Where are we going?" asks Littie as we climb into the bus.

I wave the piece of paper with Grandpa Mortimer

Felix's phone number and address at her. "Grandpa Felix's house. Where else?"

I find two seats together at the back of the bus and slide into the one by the window. Littie stands in the aisle. "How do you know for sure that man on the phone was your grandpa?" she says. "He hung up on you."

"So? Aren't you going to sit down?"

She shakes her head at me. "So, that doesn't seem like a very grandpa thing to do."

Even Littie's worst thinking can't bother me now. "He probably just doesn't like to talk on the phone. There are people out there in the world like that, you know."

Littie says, "Humph," and then nothing else.

"The bus driver is staring at you like she wants you to sit down."

Littie finally takes off her backpack and slides into the seat beside me. She looks straight ahead and says, "I'm just saying."

"What are you saying exactly, Littie Maple?"

"I'm saying that maybe that man on the phone isn't your grandpa. And even if he is your grandpa, maybe now isn't the best time for a visit." She shifts her backpack on her lap. "He sounds kind of mean."

"I thought you wanted an adventure," I say. "You're always saying how you want an adventure and how your momma never lets you do anything. And here's your chance, Littie Maple. A real adventure is right under your nose!" While Littie thinks this over, I say the one thing that I know will change her mind: "Unless you *want* to turn into your momma."

16.

We take the bus across Portwaller to 609 Antietam Street. Grandpa Felix's apartment building looks as old as he must be. The window shutters hang all cockeyed and the gray paint is peeling off the bricks in clumps like whiskers. Long ivy vines cling to the sides and front, climbing up, up, up to the rooftop where I imagine they meet and have tea parties with the moon.

"This is it," I say.

"How do we know which one is his?" asks Littie. "The address we have didn't list an apartment number."

I shrug and point to a man walking toward the front door. "Let's ask."

I catch the door before it latches shut and swing it back open again, almost knocking off a wreath of plastic yellow flowers. "Excuse me," I say to the man. "Do you know where Mr. Mortimer Felix Crumb lives?"

The man sticks a key into a mailbox in the wall, peers inside, and then closes the door. He slips the key into his shirt pocket and pats it twice. "You family?" He looks right at me when he says this, wiping his nose with his wrist.

"Yes sir," I say.

"He's her long-lost grandpa," Littie adds.

"Up the stairs. Apartment Three-C."

Littie thanks him and yanks on my arm in the direction of the stairs. But I plant my feet, wondering about his big nose that doesn't stop growing. "There isn't anything, you know, especially strange about him, is there?"

The man's eyes get big and then he gives me a

look that says, If You Don't Know, I'm Not Going to Tell You. I go cold all over and Littie has to give my arm another big yank to get me moving.

The door marked 3C is in front of me before I know it. This time Littie does the knocking before I'm even ready. "Wait, Littie!" I turn my back to the door because I haven't thought of the words that I want to say. But I hear the door open before my brains get awake.

Then I hear Littie gasp. *His nose must be CO-LOSSAL.* I turn around slowly toward the open door. And when I look up at him, the first words that come out of my mouth are filled with relief. "Oh, it's not *that* big."

And to my surprise he says, "Neither is yours." Which is a funny thing to say to somebody you've never met before. And I think he's talking about my nose, but I'm not 100 percent sure.

I pull the picture of Grandpa Felix from my pocket. The nose on his face doesn't look any bigger than his nose in the picture. Which means that

either noses grow really, really slow or Terrible is full of lies.

Grandpa Felix clears his throat, and that's when I notice how different he looks from the picture. His eyes are dark and puffy and he's got whiskers growing in the cracks on his face. He looks like he's had a thousand really bad days, one right after the next. And who knows, maybe he has.

I hold the picture out to him because maybe he just needs a reminder of who he used to be. He looks at it and then looks at me like I'm handing him a plate of sausage that's been sitting in the heat too long. I slide the picture back into my pocket.

"Well?" Grandpa Felix says. He and Littie are looking at me and waiting for somebody to say something. Littie says, "er" and "uh" and "umm," but she doesn't seem to know what to do next.

"You're really not dead at all," I say.

He straightens his shoulders and says, "Not yet."

We stare at each other for a while, and then I say, "Can I use your bathroom?" It's the first thing I can think of. "Please."

Grandpa Felix looks at me like I just told him half of a joke but forgot the funny part. Then he glances behind him, at the inside of his apartment, and for a minute I think he's going to say no. "I've really got to go," I say, shifting from one foot to the other.

"It's not healthy to hold it," Littie chimes in to help.

He grunts and as soon as he takes a step away from the door, I pull Littie inside. "Whoa, this place is a pigsty," I say. Piles of newspapers, magazines, and pictures—lots and lots of pictures—are everywhere. I pull a few from the top of a pile next to the couch. Lots of people I don't know and places I've never seen before. Tall buildings, sailboats, cornfields. "My word. What is all this stuff? Are you one of those people who never throw anything away?"

"I thought you needed to use the bathroom," Grandpa Felix grumbles, taking the pictures from me and placing them back on the pile.

"Oh, right. I do. Where?"

He points to a hallway and Littie grabs my arm and whispers, "Don't leave me out here with him. He's kind of scary." She looks around. "And this place is dirty."

"It's not that bad," I tell her.

"What should I do while you're in there?" she asks. "What if he wants to talk to me? What do I talk about? Maybe I should just come into the bathroom with you. I'm just saying."

Then I turn toward Grandpa Felix and say, "Do you have a TV?"

"Over there," he says, pointing to a corner of a room with a worn leather chair parked in front of it. "But don't touch anything, and don't move anything. And don't *touch* anything."

"TV?" That perks Littie right up. After stepping over a couple of piles, she sinks into the chair and clicks on the TV, saying, "This is great! A marathon of *Max Adventure*!" And I know she will be fine for as long as I want to stay.

The bathroom is mostly clear of piles, except for a stack of magazines called *Life* on the back of the toilet. I pull Winston's picture from my pocket. It's the same kind of paper. "Hey," I say, marching out of the bathroom and holding up Winston's page. "Do you take pictures in magazines?"

Grandpa Felix is sitting at a square wooden table, running his finger along the corners of a stack of newspapers. He looks up, hardly interested in what I'm saying. "Humph."

I pull out the chair beside him and sit down, putting Winston on the table between us. He doesn't look at me. He just stares at the pile of newspapers the whole time. I don't know what he might be thinking of, but I'm thinking that Terrible's alien mind-reading tricks would come in handy right about now. Neither one of us says anything for a long time, and the longer I keep quiet, the harder it is for me to get my mouth to work.

Finally, I tell myself just to say something. "Do you know who I am?"

He looks at me then, right at the heart of me, and his eyes tremble a little. He nods.

"Good," I say. My mouth is just getting warmed up, so I keep on going. "Did you know this dog?" I point to Winston.

He mumbles, so low that I can barely hear: something, something, photographer.

"So you took this picture?"

He nods.

"I'm going to get a dog like Winston one day," I say.

Grandpa Felix closes his eyes and tilts his head to the ceiling. I close my eyes and do the same. Only, I peek at him through eye slits. And just when I get to thinking that he's gone asleep, his eyes pop open and he says, "Elmer."

"Elmer?" It takes me a while to figure out that he's talking about that dog in the picture. I look at those eyebrows again. "Nope, he's definitely a Winston."

"Let me see that," he grumbles. I slide the page

to him, and he gives it a close look until he and Winston are almost nose to nose. Then he smiles enough for me to worry that his stone face will crack, like he hadn't thought about that dog in a long time. "I believe you're right, Penelope. He does look like a Winston."

I stop breathing for a second or two because this is the first time Grandpa Felix says my name and it makes me feel so good, like wiggling my toes in the ocean. I watch him close. I think he must like saying my name, too, because his face gets red, especially around his whiskers. "I like his eyebrows," I say.

"Who wouldn't?" His mouth seems warmed up now, too. "I bet you've never seen a dog with eyebrows like that before."

"No sir." I shake my head. "Grandpa Mortimer. Grandpa Felix."

"Grandpa Felix," he says.

"Grandpa Felix," I say, smiling. "I didn't know that dogs even had eyebrows."

He jumps a little and shifts forward when I say his name, making me wonder if maybe his toes have gone wiggling like mine. But after a moment, he eases back into his chair and says, "Well, not many do. Not many do."

17.

We make it back to the library just as moms and dads get there to pick up the home-schoolers. As soon as we get inside, I go to the first shelf of books I see and pull one out: *The History of Great Medieval Battles*. I open it in the middle, hold it up to my face, and stare at big words I've never seen before and don't know how to say. "My goodness, this is very interesting."

"What are you doing?" Littie says.

"Pretending like I've been here all day and not somewhere else doing something I'm not allowed to be doing," I whisper. "Do you see your momma anywhere?" I peer over the top of the book and hope we aren't in for a battle of our own if Momma Maple is already here.

"I don't see her," whispers Littie. "I don't think she's here yet."

I hand Littie the book and wish her good luck. "Then I better be getting home."

Somehow I get home before Mom or Terrible do, thank lucky stars. All this sneaking and snooping and not getting caught makes me feel like I am an official detective now. And I just know that Miss Stunkel would be proud.

I'm back at Grandpa Felix's the next day, after I get Littie to call my school and say that not only am I no better, but I'm a whole lot worse.

I knock hard on Grandpa Felix's door. His footsteps are heavy and slow. And when he opens the door I say, "I'm back," and then I pick up my toolbox and go inside before he has a chance to send me away.

He stands at the door in a green coat and looks at me while I step over piles on the way to the table. I grab a couple of pictures, newspapers, and magazines from the top of each one. Grandpa Felix follows and sits beside me but doesn't say anything. He rubs his fingers over his whiskers.

"Were you going someplace?" I ask, pointing to his coat.

"It can wait, I guess," he says, taking off his coat and throwing it over the back of a chair.

I thumb through a *Life*. "That's a funny name for a magazine."

"You think so? Maybe that's why they stopped printing it."

"Do you still take pictures?" I say.

He pulls a card from his coat pocket that's got a drawing of a camera on it and big letters that say: A THOUSAND WORDS. "Have you ever heard of the saying, 'A picture's worth a thousand words'?"

"No."

"Well, there you are," he tells me.

"'A Thousand Words,'" I say, reading the card. "So you do still take pictures?"

"On occasion." He points at the stack in front of me and asks, "What do you have there?"

The picture on top is of a boy in blue-striped overalls sitting on a porch step and grinning like he just won first place. His front teeth are missing. I hold the picture out to him. "Who's this?"

He takes the picture from me, looks it over, and then hands it back. "Yours truly."

"You were little," I tell him.

"That's what they tell me," he says. "Guess I'd be about ten in that picture."

"Same as me. Well almost. I'll be ten next year."

"Is that so?" he says.

I tell him that it is so and he nods. "Can I have this picture?"

Grandpa Felix scratches his whiskers for a long time. So long that I think maybe he forgot what I asked. But then he says, "I guess so," and I tuck the picture into my toolbox before he changes his mind.

"How's that brother of yours?" he asks.

I make a face. "Terrible."

Grandpa Felix gives me a look that says, He Can't Be All Bad. So I tell him that Terrible is so all bad. And that he was snatched by aliens and he smells and that I've got a list that I'm going to send to NASA. But instead of offering his help to send Prince Stupider back to Planet Jupiter, Grandpa Felix says, "You should give your brother a break. It's not easy being the man of the house when you're only fourteen years old."

But when I tell him that he's an alien, not a man, and that we don't even live in a house, he just says, "You know what I mean." Only I don't really.

The next picture in the pile is a face I know. "We have the same picture of my dad on our bookshelf at home."

Grandpa Felix drops his eyes on the picture but doesn't take it. Then he looks away. "That your toolbox?"

"Yep. It belonged to my dad."

"It belonged to *me*," he says. "I gave it to your father when he moved out."

We're both quiet for a little while longer. I watch his yellowed fingernails tap on the tabletop. He's got some kind of rhythm going, but if it's to a tune, I can't make it out. "You know what else I have of yours?" I say. "My nose." I stick it up in the air and turn my head so he can get a good look.

"I'll say you do," he says. "Too bad."

"What do you mean? I like the Crumb nose. It makes for a good drawing subject."

"You can't miss it, that's for sure," he says. "You can see one coming from miles."

"You can?"

"No," he says. "I'm exaggerating."

"Oh."

He clears his throat. "The Crumb nose has stood out in this family for a long time. My father, that would be your great-grandfather, also was blessed with this beast."

"Is that so?" I say.

A glint of a smile appears on his face. "That's so. There was a time when I very much did not like my nose. But after a while . . ."

"After a while what?"

Grandpa Felix settles back in his chair and folds his arms. "There are certain advantages to having a large protuberance."

"A what?" I say.

"A big nose."

"Like what?"

He rocks back in his chair so that it stands on only two legs. Something that Mom never lets us do. "Many people find that big noses work better," he says. "If you want to be a winemaker, a florist perhaps, even a chef, or perfumer, your nose may come in handy."

I lean back on my chair, holding on to the table to balance. "Perfumer?"

"A person who makes perfume," he explains.

"Oh," I say. "I'm going to be a famous artist. Like Mister Leonardo da Vinci, only not dead." I let go of the table one finger at a time until I'm balancing on two chair legs and a pinkie.

"Da Vinci?" he says. "You couldn't do better."

"Did you know Mister Leonardo?" I ask.

"Did I know him?" he says. "Just how old do you think I am?"

I laugh and let my pinkie go. The chair rocks back, and just when I think I've got it balanced, the chair rocks back even farther. "Whoa," I say, flailing my arms and trying to paddle through the air to get closer to the table.

Grandpa Felix puts his big hand on my knee and presses down until my shoes are flat on the floor.

"Thanks. That was a close one. Can I have some of these?" I ask, pointing to the magazines and pictures.

He looks at me like he's not sure he wants to let them go. But then he says okay, and I stuff them into my toolbox before he can change his mind.

He's quiet for a while again, after. Talking to Grandpa Felix is kind of like waves in the ocean.

There's a big *whoosh* of words from him, words that are foamy and tickle your toes. And then, without knowing why, those words pull away, leaving your toes in the sand, dry and with nothing at all to do but wait for the next wave to come.

"An artist?" *Whoosh.*

I nod. "I have to do an arm coat for school. Coat of arms, I mean. One that has pictures of things that are important to our family."

"What have you got so far?" he asks.

"Not much. I have to turn it in two days from now, but I don't know what to draw exactly. Besides, I've been kind of busy trying to find you." When Grandpa Felix doesn't say anything, I keep on talking. "My arm coat, when I finish it, might get to be at the Portwaller-in-Bloom Spring Festival. That's a festival at my school where lots of people are invited," I explain. "You could come."

Grandpa Felix bites his lip. "Things important to your family, you say?" He gets up from the table then, weaving through the piles to the other side of the room. "Now, where did I put that?" He kneels next to a pile and goes through it one by one.

"What are you looking for?"

"Gotcha," he says, waving a piece of paper at me. He lays the paper on the table. It's a copy of a story from a newspaper. He taps his finger on the page, and says, "Read this here."

"'Troops Follow Nose to Victory.'" I read the words twice before I get what they mean. "Good gravy. Is this about you?"

"No, not quite," he says. "This is about my father, your great-grandpa Albert. The one with the nose I was telling you about."

"Is he dead?"

"Yes, he's been dead a long time. Hasn't anybody ever told you about him before?"

I shake my head and give him a look that says, Nobody Ever Told Me about *You* Before.

18.

Your great-grandfather Albert," Grandpa Felix begins, "fought in a big war in Europe, many years ago. His unit was on a mission to find the enemy's headquarters. For seven days they crept behind enemy lines, risking capture. If they were caught, they would face certain death."

"Do you mean Graveyard Dead?" I say, drawing my finger across my throat.

Grandpa Felix nods slowly. "I do indeed."

"My word."

He holds the newspaper close to his face and reads: "'On a cold November evening, PFC Crumb . . .'"

"PFC? I thought his name was Albert."

"His name *was* Albert. PFC means 'private first class,'" he explains, looking at me over the paper. "It's a rank. Kind of like a title. You know, mister, miss, that sort of thing. But for the army."

"Never heard of it," I say, shrugging.

"May I continue?" he asks. I nod, and he goes on. "'On a cold November evening, PFC Crumb, out scouting alone in hedgerows near Paris, caught a whiff of a delicious smell that was unfamiliar to his sensitive nostrils.'"

"Huh?"

Grandpa Felix says, "He smelled food cooking."

"Oh. What kind of food?"

He puts down the newspaper. "How much do you plan on interrupting me?"

"That's all," I say. "Go ahead."

Grandpa Felix eyeballs me like he's waiting for me to say something else. But I just sit all good and quiet and wait for him to go on. He does. "Now, where was I? Let's see." He taps his fingers on the table again and then says, "Right. Here we are: '. . . unfamiliar to his sensitive nostrils. Crumb followed his nose to a knoll and hid there until nightfall, where just beyond lay the enemy's headquarters.'"

A gasp comes out of my mouth just then. Grandpa Felix pauses, gives me a look, and I press my lips together tight. He continues: "'When Crumb returned the next morning to rejoin his own troops, he was able to recount the enemy's exact location, enabling the capture of more than one hundred German soldiers and helping to turn the battle in favor of the Allies.'"

I don't understand that part, and Grandpa Felix must be able to tell because he says, "He sniffed out the bad guys."

"Good gravy."

"'When asked how he knew it was the enemy's cooking he smelled, Crumb said, "After day in and day out of bean rations, I just knew this had to be something from the other side. As it turns out, the

German's *rinderbraten* smells something like my aunt Becky's meat loaf."'" When Grandpa Felix finishes reading, he places the paper back on the table.

"Let me get this straight," I say. "The Crumb nose has smelling powers?"

"Well, not exactly."

"But you said that Great-grandpa, umm . . ." I pat the paper with my hand.

"Albert."

"Right, Albert," I say. "You said that his nose smelled cooking. And that made him a war hero."

"Well, yes," he says, nodding. "That's what happened."

I'm up and out of the chair then. "So I'm like a superhero?"

"I wouldn't say that exactly."

"Why not? This is a Crumb nose," I tell him, pointing to it. "Same as yours. Same as Great-grandpa Albert's."

"It is," he says.

I put my hands on my hips. "Then a super nose is what I have." And before he can tell me any different, I stick my nose in the air and try to see what I can smell. I sniff so hard I can almost suck up the stripes off the wallpaper, the dust off the lamps, the ink off the newspaper. I follow my nose around the room and holler out whatever smell crosses my path. "Old paper! Dust! More old paper!"

Grandpa Felix yells, "Be careful now!" And he is out of his chair, laughing.

"All right," I say. And when I turn to look at him, I see my dad in his face. For the first time, I have real proof that Dad was here. That startles me and the next thing I know, my foot catches the edge of a pile, the one with a picture of a cornfield lying on top, and I'm tripping and falling, knocking over one pile, then another, and another, doing a nosedive until I hit the floor face-first.

19.

I've never been to a hospital before (not counting when I was born on account of the fact that my brains were too small to remember). I haven't been here long, but it's long enough to know that I don't like it one bit. Grandpa Felix doesn't like it much either.

"I hate the way hospitals smell," he says, while we wait to see the doctor in the emergency room. His leg is bouncing like it's running a race that the rest of him forgot to enter.

I take off the bag of frozen peas Grandpa gave

me and try to sniff. But nothing gets through. "I can't smell anything."

"Keep that on there," Grandpa Felix tells me. "It will help keep the swelling down."

"Swelling!"

"How does it feel?" he asks.

"Like an iceberg." I take off the peas again and then wipe under my nose. "At least it's not bleeding anymore."

Both Grandpa's legs are going now. "I really don't like hospitals."

"You don't look so good," I say. "Want me to get you a magazine?"

He shakes his head. We watch other people, people without frozen peas on their faces, drift into the waiting room. "The last time I was in a hospital was with your father," says Grandpa Felix.

"When he died," I say, nodding.

He leans forward in his seat. "No, when he was born." He rubs his head. "I wasn't here when he got sick. I couldn't help him."

I reach my arm around his shoulders, like he's the one who's hurt. "I couldn't help him either. Nobody could."

Grandpa clears his throat and gets to his feet, shrugging off my arm. "I'm afraid there's no getting around it," he says. "I'm going to have to call your mother."

"Oh, come on. Don't say a thing like that," I say, tossing the peas onto his chair. "See, I'm fine. Let's just go." I get up and pull on his arm.

For a second he looks like he'll say, "Okay, my little darling, let's go." But then a lady with a clipboard pushes open the door to the waiting room and says, "Crumb? Penelope Crumb?"

She makes us follow her through a set of doors, down a hallway, and into a little room that has shower curtains for walls. She helps me onto a bed and tells me she'll be right back. Grandpa Felix takes off his coat and sits in the chair next to my bed.

The push buttons on the bed keep me busy for a while, until Grandpa Felix tells me that my legs going up and down like a bucking bronco is making him sick. "You're awful green," I say.

"I'm going to step outside for a minute," he says. "Get some air."

I give him a look that says, You're Coming Back, Aren't You? but I don't know if he sees me because the lady with the clipboard gets in the way and makes me stop pushing the buttons. She points to her name tag. "My name is Margaret. So, you bumped your nose, dear? Tell me how this happened."

"Do people call you Marge?" I ask.

"Not if they want me to answer," she says.

"Oh," I say. "Because the name Marge sort of looks like Margaret, only shorter. Kind of like Penny is short for Penelope. But I don't like to be called Penny."

"Good to know," says Margaret not Marge, writing something on a folder.

"The reason I asked," I explain, "is because my best friend, Patsy Cline, has an eyebrow named Marge. Your eyebrows don't look like Marge, though. They look more like a Wendy."

Margaret not Marge raises her Wendys at me and then writes some more.

"Patsy Cline, my best friend that I was telling you about," I say, "is mad at me now, though. On account of the fact that I'm a defacer. She's in this All-Star Kids singing contest in a couple of days. Did I tell you she was a singer?"

Margaret doesn't answer and instead asks me a lot of questions while she looks at my nose. I try to be brave and keep my eyes on the door for Grandpa Felix. "Is it swollen?" I ask.

"There's a little swelling," she says.

"I can't smell anything."

"That's normal," she says.

"Not for me," I tell her. "Not for this nose."

She laughs. Which I think is kind of a rude thing to do to somebody you hardly know and who is having the kind of day that lands you in the hospital.

"Can you go see if my grandpa is out there? I think maybe he forgot which shower curtain I'm in."

Before she leaves, she takes my bag of peas away

and gives me a cold pack wrapped in a white cloth. As she lays it across my nose I wonder how I'm going to keep this secret from my mom.

A long while later, the buttons on my bed have stopped being fun. I don't know where Grandpa Felix has gone to, and Margaret not Marge has disappeared. Which makes me start to worry. I don't know if they've forgotten about me, or if my nose is defaced forever. And what does that mean for my nose powers? "Hello! Hello!" I yell. "Somebody needs to fix my nose!"

A man in a white coat pulls back my shower curtain. He tells me that his name is Dr. Linus and to please be quiet because I'm upsetting the other patients.

"Is my grandpa out there?" I ask.

"I didn't see anyone," he says. "I'll check in a moment, okay?" He lifts up the cold pack.

"This is no ordinary nose," I say. "I can't smell anything. It's broken and needs to be fixed."

He touches my nose and wiggles it gently. "Well, it isn't broken. Just bruised," he says, smiling.

"But it is broken! The smeller doesn't work." I sniff at him. "Nothing."

"You've got some swelling," he says, "so that's probably why. Don't worry, it's not permanent."

The shower curtain opens again, and this time it's Margaret not Marge. But she doesn't have Grandpa Felix with her. She has my mom. And Terrible's right behind her.

"Penelope!" Mom's face has worry rubbed all over it. "Are you all right? What happened?"

I try to smile, but it hurts. "My nose ran into the floor."

That makes Dr. Linus smile, but then he sees the look on my mom's face that says, You Had Me Scared to Death, so he stops. Terrible keeps staring at me, and I'm waiting for him to say something about my swollen, big nose. But he doesn't.

"She's going to be fine," Dr. Linus tells Mom. "She should see her regular doctor in a few days just to make sure her nose is healing properly. Keep ice on it, Penelope. And don't worry, your old nose should return in a couple of days."

Mom thanks Dr. Linus and pats my knee. "Come on, let's get you home."

"What about Grandpa?" I say. "We can't leave without him. He doesn't like hospitals."

Mom reaches for my hand.

"No! We can't leave without Grandpa." I fight back the tears.

"He's gone," says Mom.

"He is not gone!" I tell her, pulling away. I point to the chair. "His coat is right there!" My voice cracks, and then I start to cry.

Mom sits beside me in the bed and takes my hand in hers. She looks at me, right at the heart of me. "I don't want your feelings to be hurt, Penelope. But you should know that you cannot depend on Grandpa Felix." She strokes my hair with her finger. "After your father died, Grandpa Felix didn't want to see us. That was his choice. We needed him, and he left. Just like he did today."

"So did Dad leave us," I tell her, "and you're not mad at him."

"That's different, Penelope."

"Well, maybe he has a reason why he left," I say. "Maybe if you just talked to him."

"There aren't words," she says. "I wouldn't know what to say to him after all this time." She wipes the tears from my face and then from hers, and wraps her arms around me. She pulls me close, pressing her cheek against my head. I can feel her heart beating.

I think about seeing Dad in Grandpa Felix's face. Proof that he was here. "I want to talk about Dad more."

"All right," she says. "Shhh now. It's going to be all right."

Over her shoulder, Terrible stares at us from the other side of the room. He gives me a smile, one that I haven't seen on his face in a long time. And it says that my brother is back, at least for now.

20.

I want to call Grandpa Felix," I tell my mom as soon as we get home.

She gives me a look that says, Don't Even Think about It. And then she tells me I'm to stay on the couch with ice on my face and not to get up for any reason. She also says that if I think she's kidding I should just try her, missy.

Staying on the couch at first sounds pretty good because I pretend the couch is a pirate ship and I'm out at sea with eels all around me. The scary kind that can shoot electricity out of their eyeballs and turn your insides to soup. "Arrr! Would be a mighty fine day at sea, matey, if it weren't for those blasted eels!" I say to Terrible.

Only, Terrible doesn't talk pirate, I guess. He only talks alien. Because he says, "You're a dork," and then goes to his room.

After a while, I get hungry. *Pirate* hungry. I yell loud so that Mom can hear me all the way in the laundry room, "Ahoy! Bring me some grub, ya cockroach!"

And when she appears with her hands on her hips and calls me "missy" again, I know that's the end of my pirate life. "Can I at least call Patsy Cline?" I ask her after she brings me apple slices with peanut butter. She tells me fine but then says that just because I'm injured and she's bringing me snacks doesn't mean she's forgotten about how much trouble I'm in after not going to school for two days and sneaking around like I've been.

I tell her that I know she would never forget anything as important as that, and she gives me a look that says, Don't Be Smart. Which I really wasn't being.

"What's the matter with your voice?" Patsy Cline asks me when I call her up. "You sound funny."

"My nose is broke," I tell her.

"You have a broken nose?"

"Not broken, just broke. I fell on top of it. And now I have to keep ice on my nose to keep it from swelling up to the size of Jupiter."

"You're just saying that so I'll feel sorry for you and won't be mad at you anymore."

"Am not," I say. "But I did have to go to the hospital."

"Stop your fibbing," she says.

"There was blood coming out of my nose holes and everything."

"Penelope."

"True blue."

Patsy Cline doesn't say anything for a while. But I know she's still there because I can hear the video of her from her last singing contest playing in the background. And her mom telling her to smile with her eyes at the people in the audience. Patsy Cline always says smiling with her eyes would be a lot easier if they had lips and teeth. "I've got to go," she says. "Mom wants me to meet with some people who'll take pictures of me so I can get more singing jobs. You're still coming to All-Star Kids, aren't you?"

I tell her that I'll come if she's not mad at me, and she says she won't be mad if I come, so we're back to being best friends again, thank lucky stars. And then I say, "Wait a minute, did you say you want someone to take pictures of you?"

"Not me, my mom does."

"Patsy Cline," I say, "I know the best person for the job."

I tell her all about Grandpa Felix and his picture-taking business but leave out the part about Winston because he has a tail. Right after I hang up, Littie plops on the couch beside me. Her eyes get great big when she sees my nose. "You look like your face has been stampeded by an African rhinoceros."

"My face was stampeded by Grandpa Felix's floor," I tell her.

She stares at my nose while I explain what happened. When I get to the part about Great-grandpa Albert and his nose powers, she says, "Are you pulling my leg?"

"It was in the newspaper," I say, "so it has to be true."

"Do you have nose powers?"

"I don't know yet," I tell her. "I didn't have a chance to really practice before this happened."

"I hope you do," she says, "because it would stink to have a big nose for no reason. I'm just saying. Anyway, I'm not supposed to stay. I came over because I have something to tell you." Littie watches my mom pass through with an armful of glass paint jars.

"What?" I say.

"Momma found out about me and you going to

Grandpa Felix's yesterday," Littie whispers. She points toward the kitchen. "Does she know about it, too?"

"Yep," Mom answers loudly. "I do."

"Oh," says Littie. "In that case, Momma says I should say I'm sorry." Then she adds, "Even though nothing bad happened to us."

Mom sticks her head back in the living room and says, "Thank you, Littie. That's nice of you to come over here and speak from the heart."

"Well, my momma made me," she says. "That's part of my punishment."

"And Penelope will be sure to do the same," says Mom, nodding at me.

Right away I tell Littie that I'm sorry that her momma found out. But Mom says that's not what she meant.

Littie shrugs. "It's not all that bad. My momma's blood pressure went up when she found out what we did, and she had to go to bed with a hot water bottle. But it went back down, her high blood pressure, I mean, and when it did, she said if I promise not to do anything like that ever again, she'll buy me a helmet and let me skateboard. So."

"That's lucky," I say.

Littie nods. "I better go now before she changes her mind about the skateboard. If you ever want another adventure to your grandpa Felix's, let me know."

"Not a chance," calls Mom from the kitchen.

"She's got good ears," Littie says. "I hope you find your nose powers. I'm just saying."

"Me too," I say. My nose twitches just then. Which makes me think about Grandpa Felix. I go to the hall closet, which is where Mom put his coat after we got home from the hospital. When I swing open the door, his green coat brushes my arm. I pull the coat down off the hook and put it on.

I bury my nose in the collar and breathe in, but I can't smell him. I shove my hands into the pockets and pull out two nickels from one and a stack of "A Thousand Words" cards from the other. I use my finger to trace over *A Thousand Words*. Then I whisper to him, at the card, "Mom said that there aren't words. And that she wouldn't know what to say to you, Grandpa Felix. I wish I had a thousand words to give her."

And then my brains must start to unfreeze about what to do for my coat of arms because right then and there I know what Grandpa Felix means when he says a picture is worth a thousand words. Maybe I don't need a thousand words to make things right. Maybe a picture is all I need.

21.

After a quick trash-can tour, I'm in my room and I dump out all of my art supplies on the floor. I pull out poster board from under my bed, sharpen my No. 2 Hard drawing pencil, and write "Penelope Crumb's Coat of Arms" in big letters at the top.

Inside my toolbox, I find all the magazines that Grandpa Felix gave me. Real careful, I tear out the pictures that he took, including the one of Winston. Then I pull out Mom's creepy insides drawings, the ones I found in her trash can. And the photograph of Grandpa Felix, and the one of my dad.

I tear out the pictures from my drawing pad that I drew of my family: Terrible's alien spaceship and Dad's toolbox and shoehorn. I add a picture of Great-grandpa Albert as a war hero. I cut around them and lay them out on the poster board, fitting them into the shape of a shield. All I have left to do is paste them on, but when I look over the pictures and drawings, my coat of arms doesn't really look like anything special.

My coat of arms doesn't look that different from Angus Meeker's. Or Patsy Cline's. "This is no good," I say out loud. "Something is missing."

Even Mister Leonardo da Vinci agrees. "Not bad, Penelope," he would surely say. "But you can do better. You have everything you need."

"I do?" I say. "But this is all I have!"

Leonardo must not have the answer either because he doesn't say anything else. Which is very annoying because what good is having a dead and famous artist talk to you if he isn't going to be more of a help?

I read Miss Stunkel's instructions again: Discover what you don't know about your family. Make a coat of arms for your family.

I look around the room for something else to put on my coat of arms. And when I see Grandpa Felix's coat lying on my bed, right under my nose, I know what I need to do.

First, I draw a picture of my big nose, the biggest drawing of a big nose that I've ever seen before. Then I take the pictures off the poster board and glue everything onto Grandpa Felix's coat. On both sleeves, on the front, and on the back. Until all of the green is covered in pictures. I save the drawing of my big nose for last. Which I glue to the back of the coat, right in the center.

"There," I say when I'm finished. I slide my arms into the coat and look at myself in the mirror. If Mister Leonardo da Vinci was here, he would take one look at my coat of arms and would most surely say, "This is splendid work. A nose at the heart of a coat of arms. Why, that is very interesting indeed." And he would be right.

. . .

At school the next day, I have a note for Miss Stunkel. The note says I need to be excused from gym class on account of the fact that if I get hit in the face by a ball or a knee or something, I could lose my nose powers forever. That may not be exactly what the note says, but I know that's what it means.

Patsy Cline taps me on the shoulder and then shrieks when she sees my nose. "It's a long story," I say. So I tell her the short version.

"Nose powers?" she says after I'm done. "From your great-grandpa?"

"And Grandpa Felix," I say. "Did your mom call him about All-Star Kids?"

"Yep, he's hired," she says, making a face.

"What's the matter?"

"Now that there's a photographer coming to take pictures of me performing, Mom said she's going to need more time for my hair than usual."

"Oh."

Patsy Cline slumps her shoulders. "She wants to put ribbons in it."

"That's not so bad." When she says oh yes it is so bad, I say, "Why don't you just cut your hair off?"

Patsy gets a look on her face that says, I Know Something You Don't Know.

"What?"

"Promise you won't tell Angus Meeker," she says.

I give her a look that says, What Do I Ever Tell Awful Angus Meeker? Then, after she looks around to make sure nobody is watching, she lifts up her thick hair. And what I see then is a big surprise.

"I've got my aunt Doreen's ears," she says with a grimace.

I cannot stop staring. I mean, they are the most wonderful things. "Can I draw them sometime?"

"Maybe," she says, covering them back up again with her hair. "But not for art class. I don't want anybody else to know."

"Patsy Cline," I say, having a thought. "You know what? Maybe that's why you are such a good singer. Maybe you have big ears so that you can hear notes better."

"I never thought of that," she says, smiling.

Miss Stunkel says, "I want to remind you all that your coats of arms are due tomorrow." Which makes me raise my hand and say, "Coats of arms don't have to be in the shape of a shield, do they?"

Miss Stunkel cocks her head to one side. "Traditionally, that's how they are done." She taps her chin. "But if you have another idea, I think that could be very interesting."

I repeat, "Very interesting" in the direction of Angus, making a big deal out of the *very*.

22.

Patsy Cline's singing contest is at Portwaller's VFW hall. Which Terrible says stands for "Veterans of Foreign Wars." I didn't know that there are wars about singing, but I guess you can have a war about anything. A long time ago, there was a war between cowboys and Indians in the Wild West, so I guess that's why Patsy Cline wears a cowgirl outfit when she sings. She's dressed for battle.

When I ask Mom if the losers of the contest get shot with a gun or an arrow, she just shakes her head at me and rubs her eyeballs. Which I take to mean that the losers will be hanged by a rope. So now I have something else to worry about besides what will happen when Mom sees Grandpa Felix taking pictures.

In the car on our way to the VFW, we have a war of our own going on. Terrible is complaining that he doesn't know why he has to come to this dumb thing. Mom says that we need to start doing more things as a family. Terrible says he never gets to do what he wants. And then there's a lot of "Yes, you do" and "No, I don't" that goes on for a very long time until Mom almost crashes us into a telephone pole. The car screeches to a stop and she yells, "I'm not having this discussion right now!"

While all of this is going on, I'm in the back of the car, practicing keeping my mouth shut tight so the secret I'm keeping won't fly out. Which it almost does when Mom nearly kills us. I hug my backpack to my chest and every once in a while look inside it to make sure my arm coat is still there. The picture of my dad on the sleeve peeks out through the opening.

When we get to the VFW, an orange-and-purple banner that reads ALL-STAR KIDS hangs above the door. I run ahead so that I can be first. Once inside, I push open a heavy door and step into the auditorium. The place is already crowded. I go down the center aisle and look for empty seats. Mom and Terrible soon catch up with me, and we find three empty seats together on the left side of the audience. I slide my backpack under my seat and sit on my feet so I can see over the person in front of me, who's wearing a hat like a teapot, and look out for Grandpa Felix.

The lights go out before I can see Grandpa Felix or Patsy Cline. A man with a microphone is onstage then talking about what treats are in store for us tonight at All-Star Kids. But when I lean over Terrible and tell Mom that I didn't see any treats anywhere, she tells me the treats are the kids performing. Which is when I say that I'd rather have ice cream.

The first All-Star Kid (no treat) to sing is a boy dressed in overalls with a straw hat, singing some song about Oklahoma. Only he sings it like this: *OOOOOOOhhhh-klahoma!* Which makes it sound like a place that's full of surprises.

I lean over Terrible again and tap Mom on the arm. "When is Patsy Cline going to sing?"

Terrible tells me to watch it and Mom tells us to keep our voices down and then hands me a program. Patsy Cline Roberta Watson is after the kid who is after the Oklahoma boy.

After the OOOOOOOhhhh-klahoma! kid finishes, he throws his straw hat in the air, spins around, and catches it on his head. Which would be a good trick for Littie to learn how to do with the Captain Hook marshmallow hat.

Next is a baton twirler dressed in a sparkly blue shorts-and-shirt outfit who does a routine to "When the Saints Go Marching In." But she drops her batons twice before crying and running off-stage and is probably hiding in the parking lot behind a trash can. Because that is what I would do if I dropped my batons in front of all these people. Everybody in the audience claps real loud for her anyway, and I hope she can hear the clapping from the parking lot.

Then Patsy Cline Roberta Watson is onstage. I sit up as tall as I can make myself and clap as loud as I can and even try to whistle, only I don't think any sound comes out on account of the fact that I can't whistle at all. Patsy's wearing her purple cowgirl outfit, and her hair is in braids threaded with purple and white ribbons. When she takes the microphone in her hand and faces the audience, she's got her battle face on.

Patsy says she's going to sing a song called "Leavin' on Your Mind" by the dead country-western singer she was named after. And when she starts to sing, Patsy Cline (the one onstage now, not the one who's dead) has a voice that is sad and lonesome, like a hound dog calling to the moon that's gone hiding behind a cloud.

> *If you've got leavin' on your mind*
> *Tell me now, get it over*
> *Hurt me now, get it over*
> *If you've got leavin' on your mind.*

Which makes me think about people leaving, not on account of dying or anything. But people just leaving on their own, kind of like Grandpa Felix did when my dad got sick. And like he did at the hospital. Mom must be thinking about people leaving, too, because I peek at her next to me in the dark and she's got a tear running down her cheek.

Then, a flash lights up the corner of the room. And in that flash of light, I can see Grandpa Felix near the stage snapping pictures of Patsy Cline.

My heart thumps in my chest. And I can hardly pay attention to the rest of the All-Star Kids. "How much longer?" I whisper to Mom after Patsy Cline's song ends.

"Yeah, how much more of this do I have to listen to?" says Terrible.

Mom tells us to be quiet and says that if she has to tell us again, we're not going to be happy. So me and Terrible have a contest of our own to see who can knock each other's elbow off the armrest. But after a while, Mom puts a stop to that, too, when she says, "Cut it out. You weren't raised by wolves." Terrible gives my elbow one more shove, and I smile because it's been a long time since we've been on the same side.

Onstage, the war drags on and on. But when it's finally over, the lights come on and nobody gets shot or rope-hanged, thank lucky stars. Silver trophies are handed out, and Patsy Cline gets one for second place.

As soon as the last trophy is given, I leap out of my seat. Mom says she wants to say hello to Mrs. Watson. And when she goes to find her, I open my backpack, pull on my arm coat, and push my way through all of the people toward Grandpa Felix.

Grandpa Felix is hunched over his camera bag,

and I want to climb onto his back so he can carry me over his shoulders like a sack of potatoes. Because that is what grandpas and dads do. But I lose my nerve and tap him on the back of the head instead. He jumps a little when he sees me.

"Like my coat?" I say, spinning around so he can see all of the pictures.

"You mean *my* coat," he says. "You've glued all that on there?"

"Yep."

"I guess it's yours now," he says.

"It's the Crumb family's coat of arms." I spin around again. "You left it at the hospital."

Grandpa Felix rubs his whiskers. "You've even got old Winston on there, I see."

"And your other pictures, too." Then I put my hand in his. His thick, rough fingers close around mine. And in case Grandpa Felix has got leaving on his mind, I keep a tight hold so he won't get away. Then I pull at him and say, "Let's go." I weave him through the crowds, and we don't stop until we get to Mom.

All the way over, my heart pounds. I stand him right beside Mom and Terrible. Patsy Cline grabs both of her braids when she sees me and says, "Look at Penelope!" But everybody is already staring.

"It's my coat of arms," I explain. "It's all about our family."

Mrs. Watson says, "Good earth, Penelope. What happened to your nose?"

"I fell down and lost my nose powers."

Mom looks from my coat to Grandpa Felix and then back to me. Here are the things she doesn't say about my coat and all of the pictures: *Oh, little darling. Oh, my heart. You're really something.*

And, here is the thing she *does* say: "Where did you get that coat?"

"From the hall closet. But before that, from the hospital, and from Grandpa Felix. You took it home, remember?" I spin around again, slowly this time, and point to her drawing of the heart. "Don't you see all of the pictures of us? And your drawings?"

Mom gives me a look that says, We'll Talk about This Later, Missy.

So I quick change the subject and say, "Look who it is, everybody! Grandpa Felix!"

Now Mom is staring at him like his name is missy, too. Patsy Cline says, "Thank you for taking pictures, Mr. Crumb." And then Mom makes a face like she's about to sprout a tail. Which must make Patsy Cline nervous because she yanks a ribbon from her braid.

Mrs. Watson says, "Well, thank goodness that happened *after* the pictures were taken. Let's get going, Patsy Cline. And keep your fingers out of your hair." She tucks Patsy Cline's trophy under her arm. "Thank you again, Mr. Crumb. When can we take a look at your pictures?"

"A day or two," he says.

Mrs. Watson smiles and says, "That's perfect," and shuffles Patsy Cline away while holding her ribbon-less braid.

Grandpa Felix turns back to us and adjusts his

camera bag over his shoulder. Then he does some-thing surprising. He sticks his hand out to Terrible and says, "You've grown into a fine-looking young man." Which makes me think that Grandpa needs glasses. "You look just like your father."

And then Terrible does something just as sur-prising. He smiles with teeth.

This is going great is what my brains are telling me, until I look at Mom and see her red blotches. This whole time she's been doing a lot of non-talk-ing. I plant myself right in front of her so she won't have to find the words. Then I poke her with my finger, which makes her mouth open. "Uh, how have you been, Felix?" is what finally comes out.

"All right," he says.

"Good," Mom says.

Then there's a lot more non-talking. Good gra-vy. They are really awful at this. So I say, "Fine. I'll do it. Mom, you tell Grandpa Felix that he is still part of our family."

"Penelope," she says.

"And Grandpa Felix, you tell Mom that you're sorry for leaving me at the hospital and for acting like you were Graveyard Dead, even though you were not."

Grandpa Felix clears his throat.

"Penelope," says Mom. "It's not that simple."

"I know," I say, "it's because you don't have words. But you don't *need* words." I spread the arms of my coat. "Because I've got all these pictures. We're all together. Right here."

"I think I'd better be going," says Grandpa Felix.

"No, don't!" I grab his arm with both hands.

Mom grabs my coat at the elbow. "Don't do this, Penelope. Come on, we've got to get going, too." But I hang on to Grandpa Felix, hang on for dear life. Because if I let go, everything will go with it. "I'm not letting go!"

"Mom!" says Terrible.

But Mom isn't letting go either, and so we're both holding on, holding on tight for I don't know

what. But I guess no matter how much you hold on sometimes, you can't stop people from leaving.

"I'm not letting go!" I yell again, pulling harder on Grandpa Felix's arm, and people around us are starting to stare and whisper, but I don't care. I get tossed around inside the grandpa-size coat as I hold on and pull, and before I can stop it, my arms are out of the sleeves and I'm out of the coat and knocking into Terrible. He catches me and keeps me from falling.

Mom and Grandpa Felix are still pulling on the coat even though I'm not in it. I reach out to grab the coat again, but before I can get hold of it, there's a loud ripping sound that stops me. When I turn to look, Mom is holding on to half of my dad's picture. The rest of his face is still glued to the coat, which is now in Grandpa Felix's hands.

And I think my heart stops beating for real.

23.

O n my walk to school, I stare up at the gray clouds. It makes me feel a little better to see them there. Like they understand and are just waiting to scatter when things decide to go right.

I leave my toolbox at home for the first time since I found it, on account of the fact that when you've lost everything, there's nothing left to fix. Graveyard-Dead dad. Lost, found, and lost again grandpa. Lost nose powers. Lost coat-of-arms coat that is somewhere with the lost, found, and lost again grandpa. Lost chance of coat of arms being picked for the Portwaller-in-Bloom Spring Festival and because of that, lost chance of being a not-dead famous artist like Leonardo.

Gray clouds. Gray clouds. Gray clouds.

"Okay, everyone," says Miss Stunkel. "Today is the big day. Each of you will present your coat of arms to the class. I've selected a few teachers to act as the judges. They will look them all over after school and decide which one will be chosen for display at the Portwaller-in-Bloom Spring Festival. Now, who would like to go first?"

I keep my eyeballs on my desk and trace over "Math is stupid" with my finger.

"Penelope?" says Miss Stunkel. "Let's see yours."

"I don't have one," I say, without looking up.

Patsy Cline gasps and Miss Stunkel says, "What do you mean you don't have one? I thought you said yours was already finished."

"It was. But I lost it in battle," I tell her.

Miss Stunkel tells me she's very disappointed in

me, and she makes a big deal out of the *very*. She also says to see her after school, which I know means another note home. While she tells me all this I'm pretty sure I see two more wrinkles pop up on her forehead.

Then she calls on Angus Meeker to show off his coat of arms. His coat of arms has macaroni glued all over it, on account of the fact that he says his dad works at an Italian restaurant. He's also got drawings of cars and trucks on it, because his stepmom fixes cars. And a palm tree for his real mom who he doesn't see very much because she lives in Florida. Truth be told, I guess I didn't know very much about awful Angus Meeker. And after he's done, awful Angus Meeker doesn't seem as awful as I thought.

The rest of the class show off their coats of arms, but none of them are actual coats like mine.

After school, Miss Stunkel hands me a note for my mom. I don't have to read it to know what it says:

Dear Mrs. Crumb,
Penelope is a failure with no nose pow-
ers who isn't anything like Leonard da
Vinci.

Sincerely and very truly,
Miss Stunkel

I tuck the note in my back pocket and head for home. Angus Meeker gets to the front door of school just when I do. "Why didn't you do a coat of arms?" he asks me.

"I did. I just don't have it anymore." I push open the door, and he walks alongside me.

"Too bad," he says.

"Humph," I say and then nothing else.

"No," he says, "I mean, I bet it was good. You're kind of the best at art."

I feel my face go red. After a while I say, "I liked your macaroni. Yours is the one that should win." And that is true blue.

Climbing the stairs to our apartment is hard

work. Miss Stunkel's note is as heavy as a brick in my pocket. As soon as I get inside, I slam the door behind me because I am an excellent slammer.

"Penelope!" calls Mom from the kitchen.

"What!" I yell. Because my nose is tingly and the gray clouds are still out there.

"Come here, please," she says.

"What for?" I say, seeing if I can make my footsteps as small as grasshoppers.

"Penelope Rae!" (Clogged arteries.)

My word. I make my footsteps bigger like medium-size grasshoppers. When I get to the kitchen, Mom and Terrible are waiting for me.

I hand over Miss Stunkel's note. "Oh dear," Mom says. Then without opening the note, she lays the envelope on the counter. "We're making dinner, and we need you to set the table."

"Fine," I say, even though it really isn't.

I grab three plates from the cupboard, and then Mom says, "Make it four."

"Fine," I say again. And the day is so gray that I don't even ask who number four is.

Mom pinches my chin gently. "By the way, how's your nose? The swelling looks better."

"Okay," I say, with a shrug. I sniff at Terrible and cough a little at the smell of his cologne. "I can smell some things now." He pushes me away. "But I still don't have any nose powers."

"I wouldn't say that," says Mom.

"What do you mean?"

There's a knock at our door then. "Your nose might have more power than you think," says Mom.

"What do you mean?" I look from Mom to Terrible.

He shrugs and then says, "Get the door, genius, and maybe you'll find out."

"Terrence," says Mom.

"What? I called her *genius*, not *dorkus* or anything," he says. "Right, genius?"

"Whatever you say, alien." And then I race down the hall before he can catch me. I swing open our door, and standing right there, right in front of me is Grandpa Felix. "Oooooooh-klahoma!" I say when I see him. "What are you doing here?"

Grandpa Felix clears his throat. "I believe I was invited."

"You were?"

Then Grandpa Felix pulls my coat of arms from behind his back and holds it out to me. All of the pictures are there, except for the one of my dad. His picture is just gone, with only a green square where he used to be. "This belongs to you now."

I slip the coat on and wrap my arms around me. Mom is beside me then with her drawing pad under her arm and her face full of red blotches. She flips open her drawing pad and tears out a piece of paper. This time it's not a drawing of a creepy inside. It's a drawing of my dad. "I was going to glue on another picture of him," she says. "To make your coat like it was. But then I started sketching."

I swallow. And take the picture with both hands. "It looks just like him." I smile at her and Grandpa.

He smooths his shirt, which I notice is a clean one. He scratches his whiskers and then shifts from one foot to the other. "Are we going to stand around like this all night?"

"Come on in, Felix," she says. "Dinner will be ready soon."

Grandpa Felix nods and squeezes by me, stepping inside our apartment. "How's the nose?"

I don't know how long I've been holding my breath, but I let it all out in a *whoosh*. "Still big," I say.

He laughs. "Good thing."

And then when I look at my nose on his face, all at once I know what my nose powers are. And they are almost as good as being a war hero. I found Grandpa Felix, all because of my big nose. That's why he's here. "I brought you back from being Graveyard Dead," I tell him.

Then he puts both hands over his heart and takes a long sniff of the air. "I believe you did, little darling. I believe you did."

Dear NASA,

My brother is named Terrence Crumb. He was snatched by aliens and then the aliens turned him into an alien and brought him back when they were done. Here's how I know my brother is an alien:

1. He doesn't want me in his room.
2. He tells lies. Aliens are not to be trusted.
3. He calls me names in his alien language (like Dorkus Maximus) for no reason at all.
4. He's always telling me what to do, especially when Mom is not around.
5. He wears stinky cologne to cover up his alien smell.
6. He's pretty good at mind reading and knowing what I'm up to.
7. Even when he looks like he's asleep, sometimes he's just pretending.

8. The smell of his feet makes me want to upchuck.
9. He's always after my allowance.
10. He tries to slice my brains open by shooting invisible laser beams from his eyeballs.

Okay, maybe every once in a while, he does something nice like help my mom fix my arm coat and not tell on me when he knows what I've been up to. So, even if he is an alien, maybe not all aliens are bad all of the time. I don't know for sure. Do you think so? Have you met any nice aliens? I think I need to do more detective work. So don't send any scientists over to our house just yet. I might keep him for a while. I'll write back to you and let you know how it's going.

Sincerely,
Penelope Crumb

Acknowledgments

I DIDN'T KNOW I HAD a big nose until I was twelve, when an uncle and cousin pointed it out to me during Thanksgiving dinner. (Thank you, Big Paul and Joey, for that one.) I wish I could say that I reacted to the news with as much sense of pride as Penelope, but at twelve, I didn't have Penelope's unique view of the world or appreciation for such things. Most days, I still don't. But I'm working on it.

For my big nose and all that comes with it, I would like to thank my grandfather, Albert Beck. His nose is a curse and a blessing. Without it, though, I wouldn't have been inspired to write this book and discover the wondrous nature of Penelope Crumb.

Thank you to the many people who read earlier

versions of this book, including Mary Quattlebaum, and my advisers and faculty at Vermont College of Fine Arts, in particular, Kathi Appelt, Jane Kurtz, Uma Krishnaswami, Tim Wynne-Jones, Marion Dane Bauer, and Rita Williams-Garcia. Your insight and encouragement helped me to keep writing until I found the story I wanted to tell. Thank you also to my classmates and friends who read early drafts, especially Annemarie O'Brien, Jess Leader, Allyson Valentine Schrier, Gene Brenek, Micol Ostow, Gwenda Bond, Debbie Gonzalez, Jandy Nelson, and Carol Lynch Williams. In addition, I'd like to thank Alisha Niehaus for her thoughtful critique, which helped me realize that Penelope Crumb is indeed the sort of girl who would embrace a nose the size of a mountain.

Many thanks to a most amazing agent, Sarah Davies, at Greenhouse Literary Agency, for your patience and kindness. Thank you for believing in me and pushing me to dig deeper. And to Jill

Santopolo, my editor, thank you for your guidance and knowledge, and for shepherding Penelope and me through this wonderful journey.

Thank you, also, to my family, for all of your support and love.

SHAWN K. STOUT has held many jobs, including ice cream scooper, dog treat baker, magazine editor, and waitress. She also holds the job of mother to her baby daughter, Opal. Shawn is the author of Fiona Finkelstein, Big-Time Ballerina!! and Fiona Finkelstein Meets Her Match!! She received her MFA in Writing for Children and Young Adults from the Vermont College of Fine Arts. She lives with her family and two dogs named Munch and Laverne in Frederick, Maryland.

You can visit Shawn K. Stout at
www.shawnkstout.com